THE PUFFIN BOOK OF
CLASSIC INDIAN TALES
FOR CHILDREN

This book belongs to

....

THE PUFFIN BOOK OF
CLASSIC INDIAN TALES
FOR CHILDREN

MEERA UBEROI

PUFFIN BOOKS

To the memory of Nicky Arni and Funky Nanjappa

And for their children

And also for Arjun to let him know he's not left out

PUFFIN BOOKS
Published by the Penguin Group
Penguin Books India Pvt. Ltd, 11 Community Centre, Panchsheel Park, New Delhi 110 017, India
Penguin Group (USA) Inc., 375 Hudson Street, New York, New York 10014, USA
Penguin Group (Canada), 90 Eglinton Avenue East, Suite 700, Toronto, Ontario, M4P 2Y3, Canada (a division of Pearson Penguin Canada Inc.)
Penguin Books Ltd, 80 Strand, London WC2R 0RL, England
Penguin Ireland, 25 St Stephen s Green, Dublin 2, Ireland (a division of Penguin Books Ltd)
Penguin Group (Australia), 707 Collins Street, Melbourne Victoria 3008, Australia (a division of Pearson Australia Group Pty Ltd)
Penguin Group (NZ), 67 Apollo Drive, Rosedale, North Shore 0632, New Zealand (a division of Pearson New Zealand Ltd)
Penguin Books (South Africa) (Pty) Ltd, Block D, Rosebank Office Park, 181 Jan Smuts Avenue, Parktown North, Johannesburg 2193, South Africa
Penguin Books Ltd, Registered Offices: 80 Strand, London WC2R 0RL, England

Published in Puffin by Penguin Books India 2002

Text copyright © Meera Uberoi 2002
Illustration copyright © Penguin Books India 2002

All rights reserved

13 12 11 10 9 8 7

ISBN 9780143335405

The publishers gratefully acknowledge Ratna Sagar P. Ltd. for permission to reproduce 'The Singing Ass', 'The Cave That Talked', 'The Scholars and the Lion', 'The Hare Who Fooled the Elephant', 'The Snake in the Prince's Belly', 'The Brahmin and the Goat' from *Tales from the Panchatantra* by Meera Uberoi. These have been slightly revised by the author for publication in this book.

Printed at Manipal Technologies Ltd, Manipal

CONTENTS

Churning of the ocean

• Illustrated by Bindia Thapar •

Rishi Durvasa was a great and mighty rishi, born from the seething anger of the Great God Shiva. All the gods, divine beings and kings took mighty good care not to spark off the rishi's highly inflammable temper; a curse from him could be earth-shattering.

One day, strolling through the forests of heaven he came across a nymph holding a garland made of exquisite flowers. Ever-fragrant, ever-fresh, the flowers shone with the colours of Indra's rainbow. 'Beautiful one, will you give me that garland?' he asked nicely and the nymph gave it to him. The rishi held the garland to his nose and breathed in the heady perfume. Drunk on the scent, he danced through the sylvan woods and his loud singing made the songbirds wince. When he paused, he saw Indra, god of the devas, coming towards him riding on his famous white elephant. With a blissful smile on his face the mighty rishi held out the garland to him. 'I will give you this,' he said, feeling generous.

Indra, who could be very crass, took the lovely fragile thing and carelessly flung it on his elephant's head. The poor startled beast seized the garland with its trunk and dashed it to the ground. Durvasa's temper blazed and Indra cowered as rage poured out of the savage-eyed rishi. 'For this I shall ruin you! From this day on you devas will get weaker and weaker till nothing remains of your powers!'

Indra quickly scrambled down the elephant and fell at the rishi's feet. 'Forgive me, great one, forgive me!' he cried in fear. 'I acted without thinking. Please take your curse back.'

'You are not very smart if you think I'm some tender-hearted, feeble-minded fool to forgive so easily,' snapped the angry rishi. 'You're a graceless, arrogant god and I have no sympathy for you. My curse stays!'

This was the time when the world was very young and the devas and their half-brothers, the wicked asuras, were not immortal. If cursed, they could lose their powers, grow old and die. Indra returned to his palace filled with a terrible dread.

Slowly but surely, the curse took effect. The gods began to get weaker and their powers began to wane. Indra's famous palace gardens slowly turned into wasteland and all the heavens, for each god had his, began to lose their lustre.

The asuras, always looking for an opportunity to strike at the gods, saw their chance. 'The devas are growing feeble and old and their hair is turning grey,' said the asura king. 'Strike now and take over the heavens.'

In the great battle that followed the asuras routed the gods who fled to Brahma.

'Oh lord, remove Durvasa's curse,' they implored. 'We are getting weak and old and the asuras have taken our heavens.'

Brahma shook his head regretfully. 'I cannot help you, but Vishnu can. Ask him.'

The gods then went to Vishnu and begged him to restore their power and glory. 'That will only happen if you drink amrita, the elixir of immortality,' Vishnu told them. 'Only then will you be safe from your brothers.'

'Where is this amrita and how do we get it?' Indra asked.

'To do that you must first make peace with the asuras, get their help. You will need it,' Vishnu replied with a wry smile. 'The amrita lies deep within the Ocean of Milk and to obtain it you will have to churn the ocean. You must use Mount Manthara as the pivot and you will have to ask Vasuki, the serpent-lord, if you can use him as the churning rope. Churn the ocean until the amrita emerges. Once you drink it, you need never fear the asuras again.'

'But they will demand their share and become even more powerful than us,' Indra cried.

Vishnu smiled, 'That is if they get their share,' he said, eyes twinkling.

The gods returned to heaven and convinced the asuras to help them get the amrita out of the depths of the ocean. The asuras, who wanted it just as much, agreed and together they went to Mount Manthara, the highest mountain in the world. But all the gods and asuras could not budge it, much less lift it up. Then Garuda, Vishnu's great eagle, swooped down and plucked it up as easily as a kite picks up a frog. He flew off with the great mountain and placed it in the ocean. The gods, more cheerful now, went to Vasuki and requested him to be the churning rope and he agreed. But Vasuki, who could girdle the earth, was too big for the devas and asuras to carry, and Garuda came to their rescue once more.

Now Garuda was extremely vain about his strength. He strutted up to Vasuki and holding what he thought was the middle of Vasuki's body flew up into the sky. He flew higher and higher yet half of Vasuki lay coiled on the earth. So Garuda folded him into two and then into four and flew high up, and still Vasuki's tail was nowhere in sight. He flew down looking morose.

'You have grown arrogant, Garuda,' Vishnu said. 'You needed a lesson in humility and Vasuki gave it to you.'

Then Shiva, the Great God whose sacred thread is a serpent, stretched out his hand and Vasuki coiled around his wrist, small as a bracelet. Shiva carried him to the shores of the ocean and Vasuki slipped off and resumed his normal size.

The gods and asuras wound Vasuki around the mountain, with his head and tail resting on the soft white sand.

The gods picked up Vasuki's head but the asuras rudely snatched it out of their hands. 'Why should we be at the tail-end of things?' they yelled. 'We will hold the head!'

'As you please,' Indra said agreeably, and the gods lined up gripping the tail firmly.

But as they began to churn the ocean, the great mountain started to sink into the soft ocean bed as it had no solid support beneath it.

'Help!' cried the gods and asuras. 'Help! The mountain is sinking.'

Vishnu quickly turned himself into a tortoise large as an island, and dived into the ocean. He burrowed into the sand beneath with the base of the mountain on his back. Now the churning began in earnest. For a thousand years the devas and asuras churned and the ocean frothed and foamed but nothing emerged from it.

Nobody likes being tugged and pulled for a thousand years and Vasuki became irritable and angry. Burning hot vapours of venom came out of his nose scorching the asuras and they wished they had the tail-end, but it was too late. As Vasuki's anger mounted, great streams of poison gushed out of his mouth but before the world could be poisoned Shiva cupped his hands and, holding them beneath the streams, drank up the poison. The bright and beautiful god swallowed it and his fair strong neck turned blue as the venom slid down his throat.

The gods and asuras resumed their churning and after a while things began to emerge. First came the divine cow, followed by the divine horse and elephant. A little later thousands of bewitchingly beautiful nymphs called apsaras tripped daintily over the foaming waters and came ashore. Next came the Parijata, the wish-fulfilling tree. All that came out went to the gods and stood beside them. When Varuni, the goddess of wine, came out, the asuras wanted her but she too went across to the devas. Then Lakshmi, the goddess of wealth and prosperity, came out of the foaming waters and she went straight to Vishnu and laid her head on his breast. A glowing crescent moon which rose next drifted towards Shiva who received it on his brow. Finally, Dhanwantari, the god of medicine, emerged bearing the jar of amrita in his arms. The asuras dropped Vasuki's head without so much as a 'thank you' and rushed towards the divine being with red, greedy eyes. They snatched the jar from him and began fighting over who would be the first to drink it.

'Vishnu! Help us!' the gods cried out as they saw the jar pass from hand to hand, 'if they drink it, all is lost.'

'*If* they drink it,' said Vishnu and vanished. In his place stood the most ravishing woman in all the three worlds. 'Call me Mohini,' she said in a voice as sweet as honey. With an entrancing smile and a toss of her head, she glided across the sands to the quarrelling asuras. She walked among them, throwing a smile here and a sidelong glance there. Utterly enchanted the asuras gave her the jar of nectar. 'Let her distribute it,' said their king, 'it will be so much sweeter from her fair hands.'

The gods and asuras crowded around her as she poured the divine nectar into the cupped hands and one clever asura, Rahu, noticed that only the devas were being served. Disguising himself as a god he held out his hand. But as Mohini poured the nectar, Surya, god of the sun, and Chandra, god of the moon, cried out, 'Stop! That's Rahu the asura!'

In a flash, Vishnu's divine weapon, the chakra, appeared in Mohini's hand and she cut his neck off.

The asuras now realized they had been tricked—the enchantress was none other than Vishnu himself. They rushed at the devas with murder in their hearts but the devas had regained their powers. With the help of Vishnu and Shiva, they routed the asuras who cracked the earth open and disappeared into its bowels.

The devas took Mount Manthara back to its place and Vasuki to his kingdom. Then they returned to heaven with the ever-full jar of amrita and, amidst great fanfare, the precious nectar was placed in the centre of a razor-sharp revolving wheel guarded by serpents whose eyes never close in sleep. The asuras would never lay their hands on it now and the gods would never grow weak and old.

The brahmin who ate up a god

• Illustrated by Tapas Guha •

Bidhata, the god who decides the Fate of all things at birth, once doomed a poor brahmin never to eat his fill. The poor man never knew what it was like to eat till he was bursting; something always, but always happened when he was eating and he never managed to finish a meal.

One day the king invited the brahmin to lunch and the man was simply overjoyed. 'Now, for once, I'll be able to eat to my heart's content,' he said to his wife. 'Nothing will interrupt my meal in the palace.'

He bathed, put on his best dhoti and kurta and headed for the palace. When he saw the array of dishes in the banquet hall, his joy knew no bounds. There were crabs and fish and prawns, fried and curried. There were spiced banana blossoms and pumpkin blossom fritters, cabbage with shrimps and drumsticks in mustard sauce, and many other mouth-watering dishes he couldn't even name. Smiling blissfully, the brahmin sat down to eat. He had barely eaten the first course when an earthenware pot hanging on a rafter fell into his plate. He looked at the shards in anger and sorrow. 'You had to fall into my plate,' he muttered in disgust as he rose to wash his hands.

The king entered when he was wiping them. 'Have you eaten your fill, holy one?' he asked.

'No, sire, that I have not,' the brahmin said, hastily adding, 'your servants are not to blame. It's my Fate,' he said clenching his fists, 'it never allows me to eat my fill.'

'What happened?' asked the king.

'You won't believe it, but a clay pot fell into my plate.'

The king was very annoyed with his servants. 'Please stay the night here and tomorrow I'll make sure you enjoy a full meal,' he promised the brahmin.

Next morning the king rose early and went to the kitchens to supervise the cooks. He even made the fish curry with his own royal hands and when the food was laid out he escorted the brahmin to the hall. The meal looked scrumptious and smelt divine. The brahmin sat down to eat and the king personally served him. He ate the first course and then the second.

Bidhata saw what was happening and frowned. 'This cannot be, he cannot eat his fill,' he thought. 'That was decided at his birth.'

The god looked carefully around the banquet hall but there was nothing there that could spoil or interrupt the meal. 'I'll have to do something myself, and quickly.'

Turning himself into a tiny golden frog he sat on the edge of the plate. But the rim of the plate was oily as the brahmin had just eaten some fried fish, and the god slipped into the rice and curry. The brahmin who was talking to the king didn't notice the little frog and with his next morsel the god was scooped up and swallowed whole.

And so for the first time in his life, the brahmin ate till he could eat no more. He sat back with a sigh of sheer contentment.

'Are you satisfied, holy one?' the king asked.

'I am more than satisfied, I am replete,' the brahmin replied, beaming.

The king then gave him many costly gifts and the brahmin left.

On his way home, as the brahmin walked through a grove of trees, he suddenly heard someone yelling, 'Let me out, brahmin, let me out!'

The brahmin looked around but there was no one there. He had barely taken a few steps when the voice cried out again, 'Let me out, brahmin, let me out!'

The poor man was utterly bewildered. 'Who are you? Where are you?' he asked peering into the trees.

'I am Bidhata and I am in your stomach,' the annoyed voice said. 'You swallowed me along with your rice and curry. A good thing you don't chew your food!'

'Bidhata! You!' came the angry exclamation. 'You are the cause of all my sorrows! I am glad I swallowed you and I will not let you go—you will stay right where you are,' the brahmin said unsympathetically.

He hurried home and said to his wife, 'Prepare my hookah and bring me a good, strong stick.'

When the hookah was ready the brahmin sat down and began to puff, smiling widely as he drew in the smoke. The god in his stomach sputtered and coughed and choked. 'Stop!' he cried. 'Stop!' But the brahmin went on smoking as if he didn't hear a word.

'Let me out, brahmin,' pleaded the god, 'you must let me out.'

'Never!' said the brahmin, 'you are going to stay put.' And there Bidhata stayed, and everyday, with immense satisfaction, the brahmin smoked his hookah.

But with Bidhata gone, there was trouble in heaven and on earth. There was no one to decide the Fate of all things, living and non-living. If this went on much longer the world would end. The gods held an emergency meeting. 'We must get Bidhata out of that brahmin's stomach,' said Vishnu. 'Lakshmi, all mortals favour you, you should be the one to go. The brahmin will not refuse *you*, the goddess of wealth and prosperity.'

'I'm sure he will,' Lakshmi said uncertainly, 'but I'll go anyway.'

When the brahmin saw Lakshmi at his door he bowed respectfully and led her to the best seat in the house. 'What can I do for you, goddess?' he asked, adding sarcastically, 'Poor houses like mine are never graced by your presence.'

'You have Bidhata imprisoned in your stomach, please release him or the world will be destroyed,' Lakshmi requested.

The brahmin glared at her. 'Wife, bring me that stick! I'll give this goddess of good fortune what she deserves! She has ignored me since the day I was born, no fortune or prosperity from her and now she's got the cheek to come here and ask me for a favour! Where is that stick! I'll give her a thrashing she won't forget.'

Pale with fear, Lakshmi quickly made her exit. The gods then sent Saraswati, the goddess of learning and wisdom. 'Brahmins are partial to you. He'll obey you,' they said. Saraswati had her doubts, but she did as the gods asked.

The brahmin bowed deeply when he saw her at his door. 'Mother of Learning, what are you doing here in my poor hut?'

'Brahmin, you must release Bidhata, let him go,' requested the goddess most politely.

The brahmin's eyes flashed with anger. 'Wife, bring me that stick,' he shouted. 'This goddess made me struggle so hard just to master the alphabet. She never made learning easy for me, as she did with so many others, and now she wants me to give her something! I will give her something!'

Saraswati fled as the brahmin raised the stick.

Finally the Great God Shiva took matters into his own hands. Now, the brahmin was an ardent devotee of Shiva and nothing passed his lips until his prayers to Shiva were done. So when Shiva arrived at his door, the poor brahmin was speechless with joy. He washed the god's feet and led him in.

'Brahmin, you must let Bidhata go,' said the Great God.

For a moment, the brahmin looked mutinous, then he bowed. 'Since you ask, Lord of the Three Worlds, I'll release him, much as I dislike the idea. Thanks to this god, I have had only suffering and hardship as my portion. I did not even have the pleasure of a full stomach till I swallowed him. I don't want to let him go.'

'Let him out,' said Shiva, 'and I will take you to Kailasha when your life is done. This I promise.'

That met with the brahmin's approval and, relaxing his throat, he opened his mouth. The little golden frog hopped out and quickly vanished. The god of Fate was taking no chances with this brahmin.

From that day on life changed for the brahmin. Poverty and hardship left his house and when Death came calling, Shiva kept his word and took him to Kailasha.

The singing ass

• *Illustrated by Pulak Biswas* •

In a small, sleepy town there once lived a vain donkey who, for reasons known only to himself, thought he was the greatest thing on four legs. Actually he was just a washerman's ass who carried heavy loads of dirty clothes all day long! His nights though, were his own. He was free to roam wherever he pleased, but at sunrise he had to return to the washerman's house where he was tied to a post until it was time for him to work.

One night, wandering around in the moonlit fields, the donkey met a jackal. In no time at all the two became good friends and they met every night. A few nights later, when the fields were full of tender cucumbers, they broke through a fence and went in. That night, and on all the following nights the two feasted quietly on the delicious crisp vegetable.

But one bright night, the conceited donkey stood up in the middle of the field and said, 'Nephew, see how clear and bright the sky is. The stars are shining and a cool breeze is blowing and I am in the mood for song. Tell me, what shall I sing?' he asked grandly.

The jackal, who was crouching low in the creepers, raised his head in alarm, 'Oh, dear uncle, please don't! It'll just get us into trouble. We are eating cucumbers that don't belong to us. A thief shouldn't make his presence known unless he wants to get caught and thrashed. Besides, your voice is quite terrible. If the farmers hear you, you'll get a sound beating. Why don't you just sit down and eat. That's what we're here for.'

The donkey was outraged. How dare this upstart say he had a lousy voice! And that too, to him who knew everything about music!

'What do you know of music—you're just an uneducated, uncouth, forest creature! What do you know of the beauty of a starlit night? You don't understand how a night like this can inspire music in the soul.'

'True enough, uncle, but you do bray,' said the jackal. 'Besides it's stupid to sing when you're stealing. It's a sure way of getting caught.'

The donkey stomped in fury. 'You idiot! I know everything about music—scales, notes, tempo, rhythm and mood. I'm a musicologist and you're trying to stop me from singing! I'll show you! I *will* sing.'

'All right, uncle, if you think it's wise to sing when stealing cucumbers, go ahead,' said the jackal rising. 'Only wait until I have left.'

As soon as the jackal slipped out of the fence, the ass opened his mouth and a harsh bray shattered the peaceful night.

'There's a donkey in the field!' cried the farmers. They ran into the field and beat him with stout cudgels. Then they caught him and holding him down, tied a heavy millstone round his neck.

For a while the donkey lay still. Then being what he was—an ass—he soon forgot his aches and pains. Rising, he dashed through the fence with the millstone dangling from his neck.

The jackal watching the charge from a safe distance grinned at the sight.

Who's the greatest?

• *Illustrated by Bindia Thapar* •

Akbar, Emperor of India, was always surrounded by men of wisdom and learning, and the brightest of all were his Nine Gems. And of the Nine Gems, the brightest was Birbal. He was a fine soldier, a good administrator and the most talented wit in the empire. Everybody came to him with their problems—from the Emperor to the poor old widow in the city. Birbal was Akbar's favourite courtier, and that naturally made him plenty of enemies in court. Legend has it that the Emperor often asked Birbal to do the strangest of things such as finding the ten greatest fools or the most beautiful baby in the city. Never daunted, Birbal proved equal to every task set by the Emperor, whether curious, odd or dangerous. And they were more dangerous than was obvious. One displeased a Mughal Emperor at one's peril, and Birbal took good care not to. One was liable to lose one's head!

One day when Akbar was in court surrounded by his advisors and noblemen, a particularly oily courtier got up and began to praise the Emperor in the most extravagant terms. He concluded by saying, 'Sire, you are even greater than the creator of the Universe.'

Akbar enjoyed listening to the fulsome praise but at night when he lay in bed a nagging doubt crept in. 'I really can't be greater than God, that's impossible. But if I am, then how am I greater? I'll ask my councillors tomorrow,' he decided and turning over went to sleep.

Next morning the Emperor addressed the court. 'Yesterday I was told that I am greater than the Almighty. Is that true?'

The wise councillors quaked in their silken shoes. How could they tell the

Emperor it was nothing more than flummery?

'Why doesn't he ask the idiot who said it?' thought one.

'How do I tell him he is not and yet keep my head,' thought another.

Akbar looked expectantly at the dismayed faces but all he got was silence.

Finally he turned to his favourite courtier. 'Birbal, I want the truth—am I truly greater than God?'

Birbal didn't hesitate. 'But of course you are, sire,' he said with aplomb.

'That, sir, is just plain flattery,' the Emperor said with marked displeasure.

'No it's not, your majesty,' Birbal said with a straight face, 'there is one thing you can do which God most certainly cannot.'

'And what's that?' the Emperor asked curiously.

'When you punish a man, you can send him out of your kingdom. But if God wants to banish a man, he has nowhere to send him.'

The Emperor frowned and then laughed out loud. 'That, my dear Birbal, puts me in my proper place, and very diplomatically too!'

The boy who became the north star

• *Illustrated by Avishek Sen* •

Long ago when the gods were still creating the universe, Brahma's grandson ruled over a great and mighty kingdom. He had two wives, Suruchi and Suniti and they each had a son. Uttama, the elder, was Suruchi's son and the younger, Dhruva, was Suniti's. The king preferred his elder son to his younger one and was unkind enough to show it. He hardly ever caressed the little boy; all his love he kept for Uttama and his mother.

One day Dhruva went to his father's chamber and saw Uttama sitting on the king's lap. The little boy longed to sit on his father's lap too and was about to run forward when he saw his stepmother Suruchi standing near the king. Dhruva looked at her with huge frightened eyes and slowly drew back. He dared not go to the king when she was there, so all he could do was stand and look imploringly at his father.

Suruchi gave the child a frosty look, her eyes boring into him like icicles. 'Boy, if you want to be petted by your father, you should have been born my son and not your mother's,' she said, lips curling in disdain. 'Too bad you are your mother's son. Brats like you don't deserve to be loved.'

Tears welled up in Dhruva's big dark eyes and spilt over. Dashing them away, the little boy turned and ran out of the room. He went to his mother's chamber and huddled in her lap, hiccuping and weeping. Suniti gently wiped his face. 'Why are you crying?' she asked.

'I wanted to sit on father's lap but Mother Suruchi said I cannot be petted because I don't deserve it. Am I a bad boy, mother?' he asked sniffing.

A sad, hopeless look entered Suniti's eyes as she held him close. 'Of course you're not, my son,' she said. 'You are a very good boy, but you see I have no position, and Mother Suruchi has a very high one. Your father likes her better than me and so he likes Uttama more than you. This is our unhappy fate.'

A tear rolled down her cheek and when Dhruva saw it he stopped crying. He wiped her eyes with his small, soft hand and brushed back the loose tendrils of hair. 'Don't weep, mother, don't be sad,' he said. 'I promise you that I will get such a high position that everyone will look up to us.'

He rose and bowed, touching her feet. 'I'm going to do penance in the forest and I won't come back until the gods give me the highest position in all the three worlds.'

Suniti didn't take him seriously and only smiled when Dhruva kissed her and left.

The child walked through the palace and out of the gates without a backward glance. He packed up his childhood with its laughter, mischief and joy and put it away in some deep dark corner of his heart. He walked on until he came to a forest and went to the bank of the river. Scarcely six summers old, Dhruva began to fast and pray with a single goal in mind.

When Suniti couldn't find Dhruva in the palace grounds she was frantic with worry. A guard told her he had seen the little prince going towards the forest and she went there in search of her little son. She found him on the riverbank sitting on a rock, eyes closed in prayer. She ran to him, crying, 'Oh Dhruva, what are you doing here? Come, my son, let's go home. You're much too little for fasting and penance.'

Dhruva opened his eyes when he heard his mother's voice 'No, mother, I'm not too little. I won't come back till I get that position. You go home, mother.'

Suniti saw she couldn't change her son's mind and she returned to the palace, terribly afraid he would die in the forest.

Dhruva prayed and did penance day after day without a break. The penance released vast amounts of energy which disturbed the seven Great Rishis who were meditating nearby. 'It must be a god or a great rishi doing penance,' they said as they followed the energy to its source. 'How else can there be so much power?'

But the Saptarishis were in for a surprise. The source of all that energy was a little boy hardly six years old. Stunned and awed they sat around him.

'Little one, why are you in the forest doing penance?' they asked gently. 'You should be playing with your friends.'

'I want the highest position that any man can ever have,' Dhruva replied in his clear young voice. 'I won't stop until I get it.'

'In that case, pray to Vishnu, he will grant your wish,' they advised.

Dhruva now directed his prayers to the Preserver of the World and so earnest were his prayers that the gods marvelled at the child's strength of purpose.

'I think I must grant the little one his boon. Even great sages think twice before undertaking such hardship,' Vishnu said with a smile. 'If he goes on, the powers unleashed by his penance could topple the heavens and crack the earth.'

'What does the boy want?' Indra wondered apprehensively. 'Does he want Amravati, my heaven, or Surya's bright chariot that turns night into day? Does he want to take our positions?'

'I'm sure it's nothing so paltry,' Vishnu said with faint disdain. 'Your heaven, I'm sure, is safe from him. The child wants something far greater. We'll know what he wants soon enough.'

Vishnu went to the riverbank and stood before Dhruva. 'I'm here, child. Tell me what you want.'

Dhruva opened his eyes and saw the radiant god with his famous discus and conch. A trusting smile lit the young face, gaunt beyond his years with suffering. With a small little sniff he told the god his sad little story.

'Mother Suruchi said my father doesn't love me because I have no position. So please give me a position that is higher than the highest and will last longer than forever,' he said with disarming candour.

'You shall have that, little one,' Vishnu said smiling gently at him as he placed his conch on Dhruva's dusty locks. In a flash, the child's weariness vanished and his thin body become softly rounded and smooth again. 'I will place you so high that even the heavens will lie beneath you. You shall live in the abode of the Saptarishis whose heaven lies beyond the sun and moon. There you will shine steadfast and constant like your prayers, and there, as in this life, the seven great ones will sit around you.'

Dhruva looked at Vishnu with troubled eyes. 'And my mother?' he asked. 'I can't leave her alone, who will take care of her when I'm gone?'

Vishnu was delighted by the little boy's love and devotion for his mother. 'In this life she will be the mother of a king and when the time comes she will go with you to the abode of the seven rishis,' Vishnu promised.

That satisfied Dhruva and he returned to the palace. Suniti wept and laughed when she saw him—she had been certain she would never see her little son again.

A few years later Uttama was killed when hunting in the forest. The cruel Queen Suruchi went to look for him and died in a forest fire that suddenly sprang up around her. Dhruva was crowned king and he ruled wisely and well for many long years. When his life had run its course, Vishnu placed him high in the sky with the seven great rishis.

Even today, if you look into the northern sky you will see a small constant star with seven stars revolving around it.

Bhishma's sacrifice

• Illustrated by Bablee Ojah •

Shantanu, King of the Kurus, wanted with all his heart to marry Ganga, the lovely nymph in the forest, but before she married him she laid down a condition. 'You are never to utter one harsh or unkind word to me, no matter what I do. One cruel word and I will leave you.' The king agreed without hesitation and they were married. Ganga bore the king seven sons and each time a son was born, she threw the babe into the river. The king witnessed everything. He watched her each time carry his son down to the river and cast him into the dark waves but he did not utter a word for fear she would leave him.

When his eighth son was born, Shantanu followed her to the river as he always did. Only this time when she was about to cast the child into the waters, he cried out in pain and anguish, 'What kind of a vile, evil creature are you? Even a rakshasi doesn't murder her children! You are absolutely heartless, you drown your sons without a flicker of horror or remorse.'

Ganga turned and faced the king. Her face was the same beautiful face and yet there was a difference. Her bearing grew more imperious, the exquisite face grew remote and a nimbus shimmered around her form. 'Know who I am, Shantanu of the Kurus,' she said in a voice as cool as the crystal waters of a mountain stream. 'I am Ganga, the sacred river that flows through heaven and, out of Shiva's locks, down to earth. I was cursed by Brahma to be born on earth but as I was leaving heaven, the eight Vasus who had been cursed by the sage Vashishta to be born as mortals begged me to become their mother and release them as soon as they were born. I agreed and I have kept my word. Your eighth son, however, you will have. Fate has decided other things for him. Your

angry words have given me release. I am going to return to heaven with your son and shall bring him back when the time is right.' Ganga vanished and the king, bowed with misery, returned to his palace.

The lonely years went by in a haze of sorrow. The only thing the king still enjoyed was the chase. One day, hunting in a forest on the banks of the Ganga he saw a handsome young boy making a weir in the shallows. Shooting arrows with incredible accuracy, the boy made a small tight fence in the waters.

The king reined in and watched in admiration but even as he watched the boy disappeared. 'I wish I could see him again,' he murmured. As the words left his lips, a beautiful woman rose out of the waters leading the boy by the hand. Shantanu recognized her immediately.

'Ganga!' he cried out joyously. 'I did not hope to see you again.'

'I promised I'd return your son to you,' Ganga said smiling. 'Here he is. He has a part of the essence of the other seven Vasus in him. The gods themselves have been his teachers, there is no one else on earth like him. He knows all there is to know about all the arts and sciences and codes of conduct and morality. His name is Gangeya as he is my son. Take him and treat him with great care for there will never be another like him,' she said, gently pushing the boy towards the king.

Wordlessly, trembling with emotion, Shantanu took his son's hand into his own large one and his eyes shone with tears as he gazed into the boy's upturned handsome face. When he looked up Ganga was gone.

The king took his son home and in no time at all the charming prince become the darling of the kingdom. When he came of age he was crowned heir-apparent and there was great rejoicing throughout the land.

Four years passed by. One day, the king hunting on the banks of the Yamuna caught a whiff of an exquisite musk-like fragrance. He slowed down, taking deep breaths of the perfumed air and followed the scent. The path led him to the riverbank and there he saw a beautiful maiden standing by a boat. Her skin was like the dark-blue clouds that bring the soothing rains and her eyes were like a deep, cool forest pool. The king reined in abruptly. Mesmerized, he gazed at the lovely maiden who stood in embarrassed silence.

'Who are you?' he asked when he found his voice.

'I am Satyavati, daughter of the fishermen's chief,' came the soft reply.

When certain, the king was never one for wasting time. 'I wish to marry you,' he said abruptly.

The girl gave him a candid look. 'I will, if you ask my father for my hand.'

'Right, lead on,' the king said briefly.

When they reached the hut, the girl went in and a few minutes later, her father came out. He stood before the king and bowed with folded palms.

'I am Shantanu, King of the Kurus, and I wish to marry your daughter,' the king stated flatly.

The fisherman didn't look as surprised as he should have. After all, fishermen's daughters don't marry kings everyday. With a crafty sidelong glance he said, 'My daughter is destined to be a queen. You can marry her only if her sons will succeed you.'

Rage and disappointment filled the king and he looked at the man with loathing. His beloved Gangeya would not be displaced! Without another word he turned and drove off.

The king returned to the palace and retired to his chambers. There he sat brooding, refusing to do anything. Over the weeks the gloom in the palace grew heavier and heavier and ministers tiptoed in the corridors for fear of disturbing him. Glum kings were easily enraged and no one dared question him. Finally the prince decided he would. He went to his father's chamber and sat down next to him. The king was sitting at the window gazing at the forest which rolled out to the horizon.

'What is the matter, father?' he asked gently. 'Will you not tell me?'

The king could not give his son the bald truth so, sighing deeply, he said, 'My great worry is that you are my only son. Should anything happen to you our illustrious name will die,' came the evasive answer.

The prince, no fool, knew his father wasn't telling him all, so he went to see his father's trusty old advisor. 'What's troubling my father, sir?' he asked. 'And I would like the unvarnished truth,' he added with a slight smile.

The old man looked at the prince almost pityingly. That caught the prince's attention. 'Well?' he asked abruptly.

'My prince, your father wants to marry a fisherman's daughter but her father has a condition—her son must be the heir to the throne.'

'Where's the problem in that,' the prince said with a grin. 'We'll give that fisherman what he wants. Send for my chariot and the ministers. We are going to pay him a visit.'

The prince and his retinue drove straight to the fisherman's house. The fisherman looked at his royal visitor in surprise. This was not the person he had expected to come knocking at his door.

'What can I do for you?' he asked a little nervously feeling the dislike and disgust emanating from the councillors and ministers.

'I am here to ask for your daughter's hand for my father,' the prince said with cool courtesy.

A cunning look crept into the fisherman's eyes as he looked at the tall young man handsome as Kama, the god of love. 'I would give it gladly but as her son cannot be king, I must refuse,' he said. 'As the first-born you will succeed the king.'

With a faint expression of disdain, the prince said evenly and clearly, 'This is precisely why I asked the ministers to accompany me. They will be witness to what I say. I, Prince Gangeya, renounce all claims to the throne of the Kurus. I will never sit on it!'

A sly gleam shone in the fisherman's eyes. There would be no loopholes. 'You may give up the throne but your sons won't give it up so easily,' he said.

The prince stood tall and proud, his face cold as marble. 'I will never wed, I will live the life of a celibate and bear no sons!' he said in ringing tones. 'Is that satisfactory?' he asked emotionlessly.

The ministers were horrified and awed at the same time. Even the fisherman was impressed by the ease with which the handsome young prince gave up kingdom, happiness and hope.

Thunder rumbled in the clear blue sky, chasing the streaking lightning. Then all was still and in the stillness showers of scented blossoms rained on the prince's head. The gods emerged from their heavens to see and bless this prince who had taken so terrible an oath.

'Bhishma!' the gods cried and the earth shook. 'Bhishma! All heaven bows to you.'

The young prince stepped down from the chariot and taking Satyavati's hand said, 'Come, mother, I will take you home.'

When the king learnt the awful price his son had paid to secure his happiness, he wept bitterly. 'For this incomparable sacrifice, I will give you two boons, my son. No one will ever defeat you in battle and Death will wait until you choose to call it.'

Bhishma, as he was now called, never married. His father had two sons and they succeeded Shantanu. The elder died before he was wed and the younger died before his children were born. Bhishma raised the baby princes, Dhritarashtra, Pandu and Vidura, acting as regent. Never did he lay claim to the throne of Hastinapura, not even after Queen Satyavati died. He kept his oath to the very end.

The cave that talked

• Illustrated by Bindia Thapar •

In a dense green forest lived a lion whose name was Khurnakhar which means Razor-sharp Claws. One day, the lion went hunting, but though he prowled around the forest he found no prey; there wasn't even a mouse to be had. Hungry and tired, he walked on aimlessly when he spied a cave. He went in and sat down wearily. Then a happy thought struck him.

'Cave! A cave!' he grinned in delight. 'Some animal is bound to come here for the night. I'll lie quietly, hide myself, and when it comes, I'll have dinner!'

Some time later the jackal that lived in the cave came trotting up the path. But he stopped short at the entrance and, frowning, looked at the ground with sharp eyes. In the sand was a set of pug-marks. 'Footprints going in but none coming

out. Boy, now I'm dead! There's a lion in my cave! Better not go in before I'm sure.'

Taking a step back he called out in a ringing voice, 'Cave! Cave! Oh, Cave!'

The lion made no sound. 'Cave! Cave! Oh, Cave!' came the loud call again.

The lion remained silent. Then he heard the jackal say sadly, 'Ah, my cave, don't you recognize me? Don't you remember what we decided—that I would call and you would answer? Why don't you return my greeting today? I'll leave if you don't.'

'Oh, ho!' thought the lion. 'I'd better answer for the cave. It's probably too scared of me to greet its master. I'll answer and he'll come in thinking it's the cave that's talking.'

Opening his mouth, the lion roared out a greeting. The roar echoed through the forest and the jackal smartly turning around, ran away as fast as he could. 'It's a good thing I came up with a plan before going in!' he thought. 'Otherwise, I would have become that lion's supper! Whoever heard of a cave that could talk!'

Krishna and Kalia

• *Illustrated by Suddhasattwa Basu* •

Vishnu, the Preserver of the Universe, periodically came to earth whenever she was in peril. The eighth time he came as Krishna. Little Krishna lived in Gokul with his parents and elder brother Balarama. He was a bright and cheerful little fellow and everyone in the village adored him, especially the girls. But Krishna was a handful and his mother Yashoda had her work cut out to keep him from mischief. If he wasn't stealing butter, he was smearing himself with cowdung and ashes. His favourite haunt was the cow-byre and, given half a chance, he was off with the cattle when they went to graze. His mission was to chase the calves across the meadow and have them chase him. His mother got complaints from her neighbours almost every day and Krishna was properly rebuked and often spanked on his little bottom, but with a winning smile he'd hug his mother with his grubby hands and say, 'You're not angry, are you?'

Nobody could stay annoyed with him for long, least of all his mother.

Once, when Krishna had been naughtier than usual Yashoda tied him to a heavy stone mortar. But the leash was long and when Yashoda went into the house to make lunch, Krishna dragged the massive mortar into a grove of trees. When the mortar got stuck between two tree trunks, Krishna tugged and pulled, and laughed in delight when the trees came crashing down. He brought half the villagers out and Yashoda, almost weeping, clasped him to her bosom and then gave him a spank on his muddy bottom.

Not long after, the cowherds decided to leave Gokul and settle in Vrindavan on the banks of the river Yamuna. Krishna loved his new home. Spring, it seemed, was always here. There were mango and kadam groves to play in, the river to swim in and wide

grassy fields to run in with the wind in one's face. There was a joyousness in Vrindavan that lightened every heart. Even the adults went about their work with a lilting song on their lips.

But this Eden was soon going to get its snake. A huge black serpent called Kalia decided he liked the balmy air in Vrindavan. He arrived there with his wives and a gaggle of children and settled down in the cool green waters of the Yamuna. Now the only happy people in Vrindavan were Kalia and his family for their venom poisoned everything in the vicinity. The fishes and frogs and turtles died because the water was poisonous. The trees on the banks withered and any animal that drank the waters soon lost its life. Even the birds who flew over the waters perished, falling into the river with a soft, sad splash as they died.

The people of Vrindavan were no longer happy and gay. Cows and calves were dying by the score and everyone was afraid of the snake. The children were forbidden to go out of the village, putting an end to all the merry sport in the cool waters. Krishna decided that this reign of terror must end. 'I'm going to kill Kalia, he killed my little brown calf,' Krishna informed his alarmed mother and before she could stop him he was out of the house.

'Oh stop him! That Krishna is surely going to die!' the cowherds cried when they saw the little boy streaking towards the river, his yellow robes billowing like sunlit clouds.

Krishna plunged into the water and found Kalia curled up comfortably on the soft river-bed. The serpent reared, weaving its terrible head but Krishna leapt on to it stomping with all his might. Kalia, writhing, thrashed the waters and his head rose above the white-crested billows. Krishna leapt around, literally dancing on the serpent's fearsome head and laughed as it tried to shake him off. Then Krishna stomped so hard that Kalia vomited blood and his fangs flew out of his jaws.

The people huddling on the banks feared the worst; Kalia would kill him. Horrified they watched the little boy grapple and wrestle with the snake and then they heard Kalia pleading, 'Enough, enough, please stop!'

The people cheered wildly as Krishna's feet slowed down. 'I'm going to kill you for all the harm you've caused,' he said angrily to the snake.

'Why do you want to kill me when I'm only doing what I must?' Kalia asked sadly. 'I did not choose to be this, nature made me this way. Why punish me for that?'

Krishna was a very reasonable little boy and never unjust. He knew that if he killed this deadly, poisonous snake, he would be doing a great wrong. The poor snake couldn't help being poisonous.

'I'll spare you if you go away from here,' he said in a gentler voice. 'And take your family with you.' Then he leapt off the snake's head and ran into his weeping mother's outstretched arms.

Kalia left the Yamuna and went to live in the great ocean that lay far away in the south and never came back to Vrindavan. And the riverbank resounded with chidren's laughter once again.

The man from Kabul

• Illustrated by Bindia Thapar •

A man from Kabul went to India. He knew just a few words of Hindustani but that didn't stop him from seeing the sights. One day, strolling in the bazaar he saw a sweetmeat shop. Now the man from Kabul loved sweets and since he didn't speak the language, he pointed to a pile of confectionery. He wanted to know the price.

The vendor however thought he wanted to know the name of the sweet. 'Khaaja', he said with a smile.

Now 'Khaaja' also means 'eat up' in Hindustani and

the man from Kabul knew the meaning of that word all right. Beaming happily, he took a handful of sweets and ate them up. As he turned to leave, the vendor said, 'Sir, you have to pay for those sweets.'

The man from Kabul bowed, smiled sweetly and left. He hadn't understood a word of that sentence.

The furious vendor went to the police who promptly arrested the man from Kabul. The chief of police gave him a stern look. 'Shave his head, paint it black, put him on an ass and parade him through the town,' he ordered. 'And have the drummers accompany you. Let the people see how a thief is punished!' he said giving the man a hard look. The man from Kabul beamed back; he hadn't understood a word.

The policemen did as ordered but the man from Kabul had them really puzzled. Instead of looking ashamed and sorry as he rode through the town, the man from Kabul smiled happily, waving at the people who lined the streets.

After a few days the man went home to Kabul. 'How did you like India? Did you have a good time?' asked his neighbours.

'I had a terrific time,' said the man. 'The people there are very generous. They give you so many things for free. Point to a pile of sweets and they say "eat up". Can you believe that? Their policemen too are so kind—they give you a shave, anoint your head, mount you on a nice donkey and take you for a ride through the town. They even had drummers for me! What a great country, what hospitable people! You should go too.'

Durvasa's boon

• Illustrated by Rajit Banerjee •

King Shurasena had many children and, out of compassion, gave his daughter to his cousin King Kuntibhoja, who was childless. The baby was named Kunti.

The child grew into a lovely young girl, serene and sensible way beyond her tender years and the king loved her dearly. One day the powerful Rishi Durvasa, renowned for his extremely short temper paid the king a visit. The tall, fierce-eyed rishi strode into the court like he owned it, with his disciples following meekly in his wake. All, including the king, rose and bowed low, heads bent, palms folded.

'O dear, oh dear!' thought the king, saying, 'You are welcome, great one.'

Durvasa nodded benignly. 'I am going to stay here for a while,' he announced and the king winced. 'I don't want to be disturbed; my movements, I must remind you, will be my concern. No one is to question them. I want prompt and quick service day or night,' he said, adding quite politely, 'I hope this will not be any trouble.'

Few would dare to tell Rishi Durvasa that he was trouble and King Kuntibhoja was not one of them. 'Of course not, great one,' he said hastily, 'my house is honoured by your presence.'

'I am now going to bathe,' announced the rishi.

As soon as Durvasa and his disciples left, the king rushed to his daughter's chamber, his crown askew, covering one eye.

'What's the matter, father?' Kunti asked, straightening the crown. 'What's got you into such a flap?'

'Flap? Anybody with sense would be in a flap!' said the harassed monarch. 'Rishi

Durvasa is here and he plans to stay for as long as he pleases—which could be anything from ten days to ten years.'

'And why should that make you so anxious?' she asked. 'Sages and rishis come and go all the time.'

'My child, Durvasa is not any rishi. His temper is always close to exploding,' the king said shuddering. 'A curse from him can destroy a world, forget my kingdom. And he's very quick with those curses. I want you to attend to him personally. Make sure he gets anything he asks for, when he wants it, where he wants it, and how he wants it. Ask no questions, make no complaints. Got that?'

'Yes, father,' Kunti said smiling.

'I am depending on you to keep Durvasa's temper in check,' said her father.

The young princess was a little scared but she hid it. 'Don't you worry, father,' she said calmly. 'I'll take care of the rishi and there will be no curses.'

For one whole year Kunti waited hand and foot on the cantankerous rishi, patient and uncomplaining. Often he ordered food in the middle of the night and when Kunti brought the piping hot food, she would be ordered to take it away. He asked for fruit that was out of season, or food that was unavailable, but Kunti did her best. Every morning the king asked his daughter if the rishi was satisfied and everyday she said he was. It was a trying time for all except Rishi Durvasa.

At the end of one year the rishi sent for Kunti. 'I am very pleased with you, child,' he said flashing his rare, sweet smile. 'You deserve a boon for all that you have put up with.'

'That you are pleased, is boon enough,' Kunti said bowing.

'Well, since you won't ask, it seems I must give you something. I will teach you a mantra that will give you sons

by the gods. After reciting it, invoke any god and he will have to give you a son.'
Durvasa taught Kunti the mantra and left as abruptly as he had arrived, much to
everyone's relief.

One pearly grey morning as the sun rose streaking the sky with pink fire, Kunti
stood gazing sleepily out of her window. Idly she wondered if Durvasa's mantra really
worked. Without thinking, she recited the mantra and invoked Surya, the sun god,
who glowed on the horizon.

The next moment her chamber was lit with a dazzling bright light, and to Kunti's
horror, Surya stood there before her. Kunti quickly shut her eyes, opening them
slowly again. The sun god still stood there, smiling at her.

'I will give you the son you prayed for,' Surya said to the frightened girl.

'But I don't want a son!' Kunti blurted. 'I only recited the mantra to see if it worked.'

'As you can see it does, and my son you shall have,' said the god.

'How can I have a son, I am not even married,' cried Kunti, terrified.

'The mantra binds me,' Surya said with a hint of pity, 'and a son you will have.' His tone said, don't argue.

'If I must have a son, he should be born with your golden armour and earrings,' Kunti said, 'and I must remain a maid.' This, she thought, would be impossible for him to grant.

She paled when Surya smiled and said, 'It shall be so.'

Nine months later, Kunti's son was born, as the god promised, with the heavenly armour and earrings. The armour was attached to the baby's torso like a second skin and the earrings were as dazzling as the noonday sun. Kunti hugged her son, weeping bitterly. 'I cannot keep you, my darling, I can't!' she cried.

That night, when the palace lay in darkness, Kunti placed the baby in a silk-lined basket and took it down to the river. Tears streamed down her cheeks, mingling with the river water as she gently placed the basket on the waves. 'May the gods guard you, my son,' she whispered as the basket bobbed and floated away.

A charioteer found the baby and took him home. The child was named Karna, the one with earrings.

When Kunti came of age, she married Pandu, King of the Kurus. Pandu was crowned king because his elder brother Dhritarashtra was born blind and therefore could not be king. King Pandu conquered many lands and then retired to the forest with his queens, Kunti and Madri, leaving his blind brother in charge of the kingdom. In the forest, Pandu was cursed by a rishi that he would have no children, but with Kunti's mantra King Pandu had five sons: Yudhishthira, son of Dharma—the god of righteousness; Bhima, the son of Vayu—the god of wind; Arjuna, the son of Indra—the god of the heavens and the devas; and Nakula and Sahadeva, twin sons of the handsome twin gods, the Ashwinis.

As Pandu's sons, the boys were known as the Pandavas and they lived in the forests with the hermits and sages until their father died.

The sparrow's revenge

• Illustrated by Pulak Biswas •

A very long time ago, in a small village on the bank of a river, lived a young sparrow who had never seen rain. In all the three years of his life, the storm clouds in the sky had brought no rain. He often heard people talking about 'rain', praying for it, and he wondered what this rain was.

That year too the rains didn't come. The wells and ponds dried up and the river turned into a muddy little stream. The people were at their wits' end. There was no food left and they couldn't grow any—the fields hadn't been tilled for years.

'What will we do now?' the people wailed.

'Make an effigy of a man and sacrifice it to the rain god,' an old woman suggested. 'That might please him enough to send the rains.'

With nothing left to lose, the villagers made a huge effigy of a man and, as the priests chanted sacred mantras, they set it on fire. The effigy blazed and crackled, and the smoke rose to the heavens carrying their prayers to the god. The rain god was pleased and sent his dark water-laden clouds to the village. As the effigy collapsed, the first heavy drops of rain began to fall.

'It's raining! It's raining!' the people cried out in joy, dancing and prancing in the rain.

'It's raining, it's pouring, Ramu pulled off her nose ring!' chanted the children as they jumped in the puddles and played catch-me-if-you-can in the rain.

When the first raindrops fell on the young sparrow, he looked up in surprise. 'What's this? Maybe the world has turned upside down and the river's falling on my head!' he thought.

Then he heard the cries of the children and looked at the raindrops in wonder.

'So *this* is rain,' he said to himself.

But the rain god was a little too pleased with the prayers. It rained for days without stopping. The wells and ponds filled and overflowed, the river swelled and flooded its banks and the people went into their houses and bolted the doors. But the poor little sparrow had nowhere to go. He huddled under a banana leaf, shivering. 'O dear, something terrible will happen to me. Maybe I'll die,' he thought wildly. His feathers were sodden and heavy and every time he shook some drops off a thousand more fell on him. 'Where can I find shelter?' he thought, frantic with fear. 'I can't fly with wet wings.' Then through the sheets of rain he spied a hut. He hopped to the door and knocked with his beak.

'Who's that?' a crotchety old voice asked.

'I am a sparrow and I've nowhere to go, please give me shelter, let me in,' the little sparrow said, wrapping his wings over his breast.

'Shelter!' screeched the old woman. 'Do you think I built this hut to shelter stupid little birds? Go away!'

The little sparrow knocked again. 'Have pity on me,' he whimpered. 'I am so frightened of this rain, please, let me in.'

'I said, GO AWAY,' cried the old woman. 'Go away, you tiresome bird!'

'Oh please, let me come in, just for a little while,' begged the little sparrow, weeping.

The door opened and, even as the sparrow sighed in relief, the old woman came out and emptied a pot-full of water on him, knocking the little sparrow flat on his back.

'Next time it will be boiling water!' the old hag screeched. 'Go away! Shoo! Scat! You wretched bird!' Then the door slammed shut. 'That will teach you to pester me!' she yelled from within.

The drenched little bird shivered and wept with rage and fear and sorrow. 'I won't let her get away, I won't,' he thought ruffling his feathers to dry them out. He went

out into the stinging rain, keeping his head down. With fluttering hops the little sparrow made his way down to the river and cried, 'In this terrible rain, she gave me a bath. O river, I want to give her one too. She wouldn't give me shelter, so she mustn't have any. O river, help me give her a bath!'

The river felt sorry for the little sparrow who had been so cruelly treated. 'First plug all the holes in your body, except your mouth,' the river said. 'Use the reeds growing on my banks.'

The little sparrow plugged all the holes in his body and said, 'What must I do now, river?'

'Start sucking my water through your beak,' the river told him.

'How much water can a little bird like me suck?' the sparrow asked doubtfully. 'It won't even be enough to wet her toes.'

'You will see,' the river said placidly. 'Now drink.'

The little sparrow dipped his beak into the water and began to suck. And as the water went down his throat, he grew and he grew until he was as large as a baby elephant.

'Now go and give that harridan the soaking she deserves,' the river said to the little sparrow.

The little sparrow looked at his enormous self in amazement. 'Thank you, river,' he said happily. 'If I wasn't so fat I would have danced a jig! Now I am ready for the old lady.'

The little sparrow waddled to the old woman's house and tapped on the door.

'So you're back, you pesky bird!' the old woman shrilled. 'Just you wait! The water's boiling!'

The door opened and the hag screamed in fright, dropping the pot of boiling hot water. Blocking the doorway was a huge bird. It moved forward like an advancing tank and the old woman fell back. The little sparrow went into the hut and closed the door.

'You gave me a cold bath and now you were about to give me a hot one,' he said. 'I am going to return the favour and give you a bath.' With that the little sparrow pulled out the reeds from the holes in his body and out gushed the water in torrents, flooding the hut.

The shrieking old hag floundered in the roiling waters which rose and burst through the thatched roof. They plunged down carrying the screeching old shrew to the river and the little sparrow looked on with grim satisfaction. Back to his normal size he fluttered up into a tree and saw the old woman disappear into the river.

That is why, even today, nobody refuses to shelter sparrows, not even when they make a nuisance of themselves in the eaves and roof. They don't want to risk the revenge of a sparrow.

The scholars and the lion

• *Illustrated by Ajanta Guhathakurta* •

There were once four brahmin scholars who were the best of friends. Three of them were very learned indeed; they had mastered every art and science. The fourth, however, wasn't much of a scholar, but he did have one thing the others didn't—a great deal of good common sense.

One day one of the scholars said, 'What's the use of all this knowledge if we don't use it to earn great wealth? Let's travel to other lands, seek the favour of kings, and earn the fortune we rightly deserve.'

The four scholars set out on their journey in high spirits. They hadn't gone far when the eldest scholar stopped and said, 'The youngest has no learning to speak of. All he has is a bit of practical horse-sense which won't gain him the favour of kings. Why should we share what we'll get with him? I vote we send him back.'

'Yes, I too think he should return,' said the second. 'Common sense is of no use to kings.'

But the third scholar was a nicer person.

'This is no way to treat our childhood friend,' he said. 'The four of us have been together since we

were children. You come with us,' he said to the youngest, 'we'll share the fortune we earn equally.'

The four scholars went on without further argument. After a few days, they came to a dense forest and walking down a beaten track, they came upon the skin and bones of a dead lion.

They stopped and one of them said, 'Here's a chance to prove how great our learning is. There lies a dead creature. Let's bring it back to life.'

'I know how to put the bones together to make the skeleton,' said the first.

'I can fill the skin with flesh and blood,' said the second.

'And I can give it the breath of life,' said the third.

The fourth, who was no scholar, looked keenly at the skin but said nothing.

The first scholar made the skeleton out of the bones, the second covered it with flesh and blood and hide, but just as the third scholar was going to give it life, the youngest, who had only common sense, said, 'Don't do that! This animal is a lion. Give it life and it will kill us all.'

'You fool! Don't try to stop me from using my great knowledge just because you're afraid!' snapped the learned scholar.

'That I am,' came the prompt retort. 'Go ahead and do what you want, only wait until I've climbed a tree.'

The three learned brahmins laughed as the fourth scrambled up a tree. Then the third brahmin bent and breathed life into the lion.

The beast rose, shook its great mane and pouncing on the three scholars killed them all. Then it padded off majestically into the forest.

The fourth brahmin made sure the lion had gone before he climbed down. He looked sadly at his learned friends lying dead and went back to the city, thankful that he had common sense and not fine wisdom.

Krishna and Rukmini

• *Illustrated by Suddhasattwa Basu* •

King Bhishmaka of Vidarbha had one daughter—Rukmini—and she was the joy of his life. She was so radiantly beautiful that even the apsaras of Indra's court turned green with envy when they saw her. Ever since she was a little girl Rukmini adored Krishna, the handsome cowherd from Vrindavan who turned out to be the prince of the Yadavas. Not that she'd ever seen him, his kingdom lay far away, but the whole world knew of his daring adventures and his extraordinary charm. Every exploit of her hero was faithfully related to her by her companions and, true or not, Rukmini listened with eyes glowing like lotus buds in the moonlight.

But Rukmini's brother Rukmi hated Krishna. He considered him an upstart cowherd who didn't know his place. Rukmi liked people who were 'somebody', like Jarasandha, the loathsome Emperor of Magadha and his equally loathsome crony Sisupala, the King of Chedi.

One day when the court was assembled, a messenger rushed in, all excited. Hardly stopping to bow in the proper manner, he approached the king. 'Krishna has killed Kansa! The tyrant is dead and the Yadavas have a new king,' he announced.

Rukmi rose, purpling with fury. Kansa was Jarasandha's son-in-law and a very dear friend. 'That murdering cowherd! He ought to be hanged!' he said harshly.

Rukmini, who was listening wide-eyed, rose in defence of her hero. 'He's not a cowherd, he's a prince. That awful Kansa was his cousin—so he can't be a cowherd, can he?' she ended triumphantly. Rukmi shot his young sister a withering look. 'He was brought up by cowherds and is no better,' he snapped.

'You know, he's the son of Vasudeva and Devaki,' the queen, his mother, said mildly.

'They hid him in Gokul because Kansa would have killed him otherwise. He killed all Devaki's children as soon as they were born.' An expression of distaste crossed her face. 'Kansa deposed his old father Ugrasena and took the throne.'

'If you call that noble behaviour, then it's a good thing Krishna missed out on a royal upbringing,' Rukmini pointed out cheerfully.

Rukmi ignored her and turned to the messenger, 'I suppose he's gone and crowned himself King of Mathura,' he said with a sneer.

'No, my prince,' the messenger answered quickly, 'he refused the crown and installed the old King Ugrasena on the throne.'

'See! That's called a hero!' Rukmini crowed, jubilant. 'I am sure all of Mathura is dancing in the streets. That wicked man deserved to die!'

'That will do, Rukmini,' her father rebuked gently. 'It is most unseemly to show such delight at anyone's death.' He turned to the messenger. 'How has the Emperor taken it?'

'Jarasandha vows revenge. He says he won't rest till he destroys Mathura,' the messenger replied.

'I must leave at once,' Rukmi said bowing briefly to his parents, 'the Emperor will need me.'

King Bhishmaka and his queen however were pleased with the turn of events in Mathura. 'Old Ugrasena must be a very happy man,' the king said.

'Yes, and Krishna has acted most nobly,' the queen observed. 'Just the kind of young man I would like to see Rukmini wed.'

'Indeed,' sighed the king, 'but I doubt Rukmi will agree.'

Emperor Jarasandha mustered his allies and marched on Mathura. Eighteen times the Emperor tried to avenge Kansa but the Yadavas, under Krishna's able leadership, drove his armies back though they never quite managed to rout him. Weary of the long years of constant warfare, the Yadavas abandoned Mathura and went far away to a land in the west. There they built a great city, so well fortified that a handful of women could easily defend it. Stories of Krishna's valour and daring were the topic of conversation everywhere and Rukmini's love and admiration grew with each passing season. Each time Krishna was mentioned, Rukmini's face would light up, much to her brother's displeasure.

One day the king and Rukmi were walking in the palace garden discussing Rukmini's future. They didn't notice Rukmini sitting in the jasmine bower and she overhead everything they said.

'It is time Rukmini was wed,' the king stated. 'Your mother and I have decided to give her to Krishna.'

'Never!' Rukmi said flatly. 'I'll never allow her to marry that wretched Yadava cowherd. I will give her to Sisupala of Chedi.'

Rukmini turned as pale as the jasmines she was holding but her eyes flashed. 'I'll never marry that jackal! Oh Rukmi how can you do this to me just to gain the Emperor's favour?' she thought. 'Oh father don't let him persuade you.'

As if on cue, the old king said, 'We should hold a swayamvara, as is customary. Rukmini should be allowed to choose her own husband.'

'There will be no swayamvara,' Rukmi said tersely. 'She'll only put the garland around that cowherd's neck and she must not be given a chance to do that.'

The old king usually let Rukmi make the final decision. 'Do what you think is best,' he said heavily.

Rukmini sat down, sobbing softly, 'What can I do? I won't marry that vile man!' Then the tears stopped and her eyes shone. 'I'll write to Krishna, ask him to carry me away! And I don't care if it's not the done thing!' she thought defiantly.

Rukmini wrote a letter and the old brahmin priest who had known her since she was a toddler took it to Dwaraka. Rukmi set the date for her wedding to Sisupala and preparations began in earnest. All the kings were invited and Sisupala arrived with the Emperor. He strutted about the city like a rooster with a stiff neck. 'Rukmini will be mine, how the other kings envy me,' he said to anybody who cared to listen.

Rukmini waited for an answer with mounting alarm. Would Krishna come? Would he come in time? Would he come at all?

The priest reached Dwaraka and gave Rukmini's letter to Krishna. Krishna read it with a tender smile on his lips. Then putting it away he gave the priest a verbal reply. 'Tell her I'll be there and not to worry about Jarasandha's army. She says she will go to Parvati's temple on her wedding morning to offer worship. Tell her I'll meet her in the temple complex. Now that I know she cares, nothing will stop me from carrying her away—not the Emperor, not his army, not her brother.'

'The princess begs you not to kill anyone in her family,' the priest said.

'I'll bear that in mind,' Krishna smiled.

'I must leave now,' the priest said bowing. 'The princess will be waiting anxiously for me.'

Sisupala of Chedi was a happy man but the Emperor was not so confident. 'I don't trust that cowherd. He'll try and carry Rukmini away. There's talk that she would have garlanded him had there been a swayamvara. A good thing I brought the army with me.'

As soon as the priest returned to Vidarbha he went straight to Rukmini. The princess jumped up and ran to him, crying, 'Did you give him my letter? Will he come? Was he disgusted by my boldness?'

'One at a time, my princess,' the priest said with a laugh. 'Yes he will come—he will be here any day now. And no, he was not offended by your letter.'

Krishna left Dwaraka in a fast chariot. Balarama, his brother, got wind of his plan and a worried frown creased his brow when he was told that Krishna had gone alone. 'He has always been impetuous,' he said, adding briskly, 'Tell the generals I want the army ready to march. We will be up against the Emperor's army.'

Krishna reached Vidarbha just before the wedding day and King Bhishmaka silently hoped that Krishna was there to spirit Rukmini away. He welcomed Krishna and escorted him to a mansion in the palace grounds. On the way, Krishna saw the temple to Goddess Parvati and a smile flickered in his eyes.

Rukmini's wedding morning dawned, cool and fresh. The princess was dressed in all her finery. Her long black hair was braided with jasmine and pearls. Great rubies hung in her ears and glittered around her neck. Yards of red and gold silk were draped around her slender form to fall in supple folds to her delicate feet. A golden girdle was clasped around her hips and she wore jewelled anklets on her feet. Her maids hovered around, oohing and aahing at every step of her elaborate toilette. When all was done, Rukmini got into her chariot and was driven to the temple. She walked slowly up the steps and her veil hid the fear and apprehension in her eyes. 'They say he wears golden-yellow robes, has peacock feathers in his crown and is dark like a monsoon cloud. I do not see anyone who fits this description,' she thought as she looked at the small crowd of kings and princes that had gathered there.

She went into the temple, made offerings and washed the goddess' feet. 'O Mother, please send him. Please let him rescue me, don't let Sisupala be my husband,' was her silent, desperate prayer.

As soon as she came out her eyes swept over the crowd and her heart sank. There was no sign of Krishna. Then, as she was about to step into her chariot, she felt an arm around her waist and in a trice she was whisked into another chariot. She threw back her veil and looked into Krishna's laughing face, beautiful as the monsoon clouds that come after a long harsh summer. 'You came!' she whispered, eyes glowing brighter than her jewels. 'Oh, you came.'

'Hold on,' Krishna said picking up the reins. 'It's going to be a rough ride.' Even as the stunned kings looked on, the chariot sped away.

'Stop him!' Rukmi cried. 'Stop that blasted cowherd!'

Jarasandha's eyes bulged with anger. 'Move, you dolts!' he bawled at the poor vassal kings. 'Go after that wretch! I'll follow with the army.'

Krishna raced out of the city with the kings in hot pursuit. To his great relief, he saw Balarama outside the city walls. 'Am I glad to see you,' he said laughing as he reined in. 'I don't think I could have taken on the entire army.'

'Get going, Krishna,' Balarama said shortly. 'Get Rukmini away from here.'

'Not on your life!' Krishna laughed. 'A good fight before breakfast does wonders for the appetite.'

'Don't be an idiot!' Balarama snapped. 'Rukmini could get hurt. I'll take care of Jarasandha.'

Krishna moved just as the soldiers poured out of the city gates. Balarama's infantry checked their advance giving Krishna time to get away. The brief battle was over when the kings saw Krishna disappearing over the horizon. But Rukmi cut loose and raced after the fleeing pair.

'You thief, release my sister!' he shouted as his chariot drew alongside Krishna's. Then raising his bow he released an arrow, which bounced off Krishna's armour. Krishna, who really did not want to fight the fuming Rukmi, raised his bow in reply. His arrows shattered the wheels, then the axle and finally the chariot. Rukmi rose from the debris with his sword raised and Krishna leapt down from his chariot.

'I'll kill you, you stinking cowherd!' Rukmi cried as he rushed at Krishna.

Krishna parried the blow, and would have wounded Rukmi fatally but stopped short when he heard Rukmini's anguished cry, 'No! No! Please.'

Rukmini jumped down and fell at Krishna's feet. 'Please don't kill my brother,' she wept.

Krishna threw his sword down and raised her up. 'For your sake, he shall live,' he said.

Krishna took Rukmini to Dwaraka and the whole city rejoiced when Krishna married his beautiful, hard-won Rukmini.

The magic potion

• Illustrated by Neeta Gangopadhya •

The blind king Dhritarashtra had a hundred sons called the Kauravas and they lived in Hastinapura, the great capital of the Kurus. In the palace, only a few loyal people remembered that Pandu was the true king of the Kurus. Duryodhana, the eldest Kaurava, thought the kingdom was his birthright and his father never said anything to the contrary. But then King Pandu and Queen Madri died in the forest and Kunti arrived in Hastinapura with her five sons.

The moment the Kauravas set eyes on their five cousins, they bristled and a bitter rivalry sprang up. Duryodhana hated the Pandavas because he knew Yudhishthira was the rightful heir to the throne. But the Pandavas could do nothing as they were minors and power lay with King Dhritarashtra. They tried to mind their own business and stay out of trouble. That is, all but Bhima.

Young Bhima was a great one for pranks and to top it all the gods had given him superhuman strength. Needling the stuffed-up Kauravas was an activity he enjoyed immensely. He'd shake them down from the trees when they were picking fruit, laughing uproariously as they came tumbling down. And if they tried to lynch him, he'd shake them off like little rats. In the wrestling pit he got great pleasure in rubbing their noses in the dirt, his eyes gleaming with merriment as he held them down. The Kauravas hated the Pandavas but hated Bhima most because they never managed to get even. Every time Duryodhana looked at Bhima, he could taste his hatred and when that hatred burst its bonds, Duryodhana decided to kill Bhima.

'We'll put him away, permanently,' he said viciously. 'Without him the Pandavas are nothing.'

One bright sunny spring morning when cuckoos were laying eggs in crows' nests and the bees were buzzing madly among nectar-filled flowers, the Kauravas invited the Pandavas to a picnic.

Duryodhana specially told his cooks to prepare all Bhima's favourite dishes. The Pandavas were surprised by this sudden friendliness but being good-natured boys, they accepted with pleasure.

The princes in their gilded chariots raced into the golden day. When they reached the riverbank, their attendants set about cooking and pitching tents while the boys went for a swim. They frolicked and played in the cool waters until the aromas of the food reached their nostrils. That told them they were starving. Quickly putting on their clothes, they sat down to a scrumptious meal.

Duryodhana, much to Bhima's astonishment, served him with his own hands, piling his plate up with meats and vegetables. 'See, all your favourite things,' he said with a smile.

Though strong and brave, Bhima was a simple-hearted boy. Grinning happily at his cousin he said a quick 'thank you' and tucked in.

When the princes had stuffed

themselves till they could eat no more, they got up and drifted off into the coolness of the forest. Only Bhima still sat eating. The Kauravas didn't go far; hidden in the nearby trees, they stood watching him.

When Bhima was done he got up and walked down to the sandy shore. There was a strange buzz in his head and his limbs felt heavy and sluggish. 'Maybe I've eaten too much,' he thought, lying down on the warm sand and closing his eyes.

When Bhima's sleeping form grew still as the nearby rocks, the Kauravas emerged.

'Quick! Cut some thick, strong vines,' Duryodhana said to his brothers. 'Tie him up tight. The poison is doing its work, but I'm taking no chances. With him dead, the Pandavas won't ever be able to lay claim to the throne.'

The Kauravas bound Bhima's feet and arms with tough pliable vines. Then they picked him up and threw him into the river. The boy sank to the bottom and fell into the realm of the Nagas, landing in a pit of snakes. The Nagas looked at the strange creature in their midst and reared their heads, hissing with anger as they sank their fangs into his body. Their poison flowed into Bhima's veins meeting the other already there, and each destroyed the other.

Bhima opened his eyes and the snakes drew back in fear. Then to their horror, the creature flexed his powerful muscles and broke his fetters. Bits of vine flew out, smacking the snakes in their faces. Roaring, Bhima grabbed the nearest and sent them to heaven. The rest fled.

Vasuki, the great lord of the serpent kingdom, was surprised to see some wild-eyed Nagas running towards him. His subjects were not easily frightened. They began talking all at once. 'There's a boy there your majesty…a huge brute of a boy! When he fell he was unconscious. We bit him and instead of dying, as he should have, he revived. Attacked and killed quite a few of us!'

'I must see this lad who can make my serpents quiver,' King Vasuki said. 'Take me to him.'

The king and his councillors found Bhima ringed by dead Nagas. The boy looked up and stared unafraid at the great serpent king. Vasuki liked the courage he displayed, but before he could question him Aryaka, his chief minister, went to the boy and embraced him.

'Who's this?' Bhima wondered, 'and what's he doing, hugging me?'

'I am your mother's grandfather, my child,' Aryaka said, reading his mind. 'You are safe here.'

'I'm not afraid,' Bhima muttered but Aryaka had turned away.

'Sire, this is Bhima, Kunti's second son,' he said.

'Why have you entered my kingdom?' Vasuki asked.

'I didn't come, I found myself here,' Bhima replied. 'I was all tied up. I don't know how I got here though,' he confessed. 'When I awoke I was surrounded by snakes and they were biting me. I was so furious I killed them.'

'You were poisoned and thrown in,' Vasuki said shrewdly. 'You have shown great courage, so before you leave my kingdom take as many gems as you can carry.'

'Gems he can get, your majesty,' Aryaka said to his king. 'If you wish to make him a gift then let him drink Rasakunda, the elixir of strength.'

The king inclined his head graciously. 'Boy, thanks to your great-grandfather you will receive a priceless gift.'

The Nagas took Bhima to the palace and led him to the chamber where the magical potion was kept. In it were line upon line of small jars filled with the elixir.

'Drink as much as you can,' Vasuki said to Bhima. 'Each jar contains the strength of a thousand elephants.'

Bhima opened one jar and downed it. Then he picked up a second and a third.

The Nagas looked at him with dawning respect. Nobody had drunk more than two. Bhima emptied eight jars, and as he drank the eighth the Nagas bowed to the boy. This was truly a magnificent feat!

'Now you must sleep,' the king said. 'Each jar takes one day to digest. I'm afraid you will be asleep for a while. When you wake up you can go home.' They escorted Bhima to a chamber with a bed and Bhima fell into a deep dreamless sleep.

Back on the riverbank, the sun sank slowly

into the distant marshes. The princes got into their chariots and drove back to the city. On the way Yudhishthira noticed that Bhima was missing.

'Where's Bhima?' he asked Arjuna.

'He's probably gone ahead,' came the casual reply.

When they got home, Kunti came out and immediately noticed that Bhima wasn't among them.

'Where's Bhima?' she asked sharply.

'Why, isn't he here?' Arjuna asked in surprise.

'Would I ask if he was?' Kunti said tersely. 'Now go back and look for him. All of you are in danger here but Bhima most of all. For all his strength he is guileless and a bit naïve, unlike the rest of you. Something must have happened to him.'

The Pandavas returned to the riverbank and though they looked everywhere, they couldn't find Bhima. Now thoroughly alarmed they went home and told their mother that Bhima was nowhere to be found.

'It's as if he's vanished,' the twins said.

'Say nothing of this to anyone,' Kunti told them. 'No one must know that Bhima's missing. And don't walk around with long faces—act your usual selves.'

Kunti quietly sent out search parties but there was no news of Bhima. The Pandavas noticed their cousins' gloating faces but were helpless without proof, so they pretended they didn't know the Kauravas were responsible.

Seven days passed. Kunti and the Pandavas were now sure that Bhima was dead. Far away from prying eyes, they wept into their pillows. The next morning, when they were sitting, picking at their breakfast, there was a shout in the hallway and Bhima burst into the room, eyes shining with excitement. His brothers leapt up laughing and hugging him, bombarding him with questions. Bhima gently shoved them aside and went and touched his mother's feet, but his mother could see he was bursting with news. 'Where were you?' she asked.

'O mother, what an adventure!' he said, his eyes dancing. 'First the Kauravas poisoned me and threw me into the river. Then I fell into the Naga kingdom and they bit me and instead of dying I became okay. Then I met your grandfather, and King Vasuki gave me Rasakunda to drink. So I had to go to sleep for eight days,' he explained. 'And I killed a lot of snakes,' he added gleefully.

His mother and brothers did not find the thought of his being poisoned a laughing matter.

Bhima grinned into their serious faces. 'Stop looking so gloomy. I'm not dead and now I've got the strength of eight thousand elephants! I drank eight jars,' he said proudly.

That had them laughing but Kunti told them to keep their voices down. 'The Kauravas will keep trying to kill you. Each of you must look out for the other. And Bhima, please don't let your cousins suspect you know about their attempt on your life. That will make matters even more dangerous.'

The Kauravas soon learnt that Bhima was back, stronger than ever. 'He escaped this time,' Duryodhana said darkly. 'Next time the Pandavas won't be so lucky.'

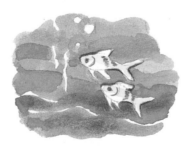

The kidnapping of Sita

• Illustrated by K. P. Sudesh •

Rama, the eldest son of Dashratha, King of Ayodhya, was exiled into the forest for fourteen years. His stepmother Kaikeyi wanted her son Bharata to be king and so she used a boon granted by the king years before to get rid of the much-loved Rama, Prince of Ayodhya. Rama left his father's city and his homeland with his sweet gentle wife, Sita, and his younger brother, Lakshmana, and went to live in the forest.

For many years they wandered over the face of the land, travelling far to the south. They saw many strange sights, had many fine adventures and made some great friends. The thirteenth year saw the exiles in the beautiful forest of Panchavati which lay on the banks of the Godavari. In the middle of the forest was a glade encircled by five towering peepal trees and Rama and Lakshmana built their hermitage within the circle. Sita, a seasoned forest-dweller now, soon made the hut a home. The deer in the nearby woods grew to know her and tamely followed her when she went to fetch water or pluck flowers and fruit.

But the forest had its dark side. It was filled with rakshasas who had all kinds of tricks up their sleeves. Rama warned Lakshmana and Sita about them. 'Not all things are what they seem to be.'

What they didn't know was that the forest near the hermitage was home to Surpanakha, the demoness who was the sister of Ravana, the mighty King of Lanka. She was roaming the world in search of a mate when she saw Rama and she wanted him. One day she waylaid him in the forest. 'Leave that whey-faced princess of yours and marry me,' she said to the hero.

Rama laughed into her ugly face and then, being a well-brought up man, told her that he would do no such a thing, he was a married man. Then the demoness went to Lakshmana and asked him to marry her but Lakshmana turned away in disgust. Her eyes fell on Sita and hatred welled up like a tidal wave. 'If I kill her, Rama can marry me!' she thought and rushed at the princess but Lakshmana stopped her charge. Furious, she grabbed Lakshmana and rose into the sky with him. Lakshmana thoroughly angry now drew out his sword and cut off her nose and ears. Roaring in agony, she let go off him and flew towards the south.

She went to her brothers Khara and Dushana and when they saw her mutilated face they attacked the hermitage, but Rama and Lakshmana killed them both and decimated their army. When Surpanakha heard her brothers were dead, she wanted nothing now but revenge. 'I will take away his happiness and desire for life. He shall lose Sita and without her he'll die!' she swore viciously.

Surpanakha flew to Lanka which lay beyond the great ocean and went straight to her brother Ravana. When the mighty king saw her disfigured face a black rage rose in his breast. 'Who did this to you?' he asked with burning anger. 'I'll kill him.'

'I don't want you to kill Rama, besides, you can't, he and his brother destroyed Khara's army. Instead I want you to take his beautiful wife Sita away from him,' Surpanakha said. 'Without her he will die, and without him Lakshmana, who did this, will die. I want them both dead.'

As his sister told him about Sita's fabled beauty, Ravana liked the idea of abducting her more and more. He sent for his flying chariot and flew off to Panchavati but he didn't go straight to the hermitage. He would need help if he wanted to kidnap Sita and so he went to Maricha, the rakshasa-magician who lived in the same forest. 'I want you to help me carry Sita away,' he said.

'Don't even think about it,' Maricha advised. 'Rama is dangerous, don't trifle with him. Take his wife and you're inviting death.'

'You are still my subject,' Ravana reminded him coldly. 'I can have you put to death if you don't obey my orders, so you might as well.'

Maricha bowed. 'You leave me no choice, it seems I will lose my life either way.'

'I want you to take the form of a golden deer. Sita will desire you and you can draw Rama and Lakshmana away from the hermitage. That will leave Sita alone for me.'

'This is the beginning of your end,' Maricha said as he stepped into the chariot, but Ravana only laughed. They flew off, landing near the hermitage. Maricha changed himself into a beautiful golden deer with shining antlers and spots that gleamed as if studded with gems. With a flash of its tail the deer ran into the hermitage where Sita was plucking flowers. Her eyes lit up when she saw the beautiful creature.

'How lovely you are,' she said softly, moving slowly towards it. 'Rama! Lakshmana! Come here quickly,' she called. The brothers came out of the hut wondering what was causing such excitement. 'Look Rama,' she said pointing to the deer. 'Have you ever seen such a lovely creature? Oh Rama, all these years I've never asked you for anything. Now I ask, get me this deer.'

Rama smiled lovingly at his wife. 'Of course I will.' Turning to Lakshmana he said, 'Stay here with Sita, while I go after it. And don't leave her alone.'

Lakshmana was looking suspiciously at the animal. 'This deer is too beautiful to be true,' he said frowning. 'It could be that rakshasa Maricha. He can take any form he wants.'

'If it is indeed the old magician, I'll rid the forest of his presence,' Rama said, picking up his bow and quiver.

With a flick of its tail the deer bounded into the forest and Rama followed. Chasing the animal through the trees, he realized that he would have to bring it down if he wanted to capture it. Rama shot an arrow into the golden hide and the deer fell, crying out in Rama's voice, 'O Sita, O Lakshmana! Help me! This rakshasa will kill me!' The deer vanished, and in its place lay a mortally wounded rakshasa. 'This is my last service to my king,' he said and died. Even rakshasas could be loyal and true.

In the hermitage Sita heard the cry. 'That's Rama's voice,' she said in alarm. 'Go to him Lakshmana, he's crying for help.'

'That's probably Maricha trying to trick us,' Lakshmana said calmly. 'Rama would never cry for help.'

'It is him,' Sita insisted sharply. 'Do you think I don't know my husband's voice?' Fear and anger made her say nasty, horrid things to poor Lakshmana, deeply hurting him. Reluctantly he went in search of Rama, leaving Sita alone in the hermitage.

Ravana saw Lakshmana disappear into the forest and laughed softly. 'Now I'll get you, you little beauty.' He made a magical sign and his royal garments and nine of his

ten heads disappeared. In his place stood a gentle-faced ascetic in saffron coloured robes and wooden sandals. Chanting a hymn, he went into the hermitage and saw Sita sitting on the doorstep, weeping bitterly.

'Lovely one, what are you doing alone in the forest, filled with wild beasts and evil creatures?'

Looking up, Sita saw a pious brahmin standing before her. Wiping her eyes, she rose to greet him and offered him food and water. 'My husband and his brother are with me, holy one,' she said. 'I am alone only because they have gone to catch a deer for me.'

Then Sita noticed that a strange, frightening stillness had fallen over the woods. No birds darted from branch to branch, twittering and cheeping. No bees hummed among the flowers and no little animals scurried in the bushy undergrowth of the forest floor. She looked at the brahmin with mounting fear, his smile making her tremble. He made a sign and the brahmin disappeared, and in his place stood a towering, richly dressed man, with a jewelled crown on his head. Sita stood rooted with fright. 'Come!' he ordered. 'I am Ravana, King of Lanka, whom gods and men fear. Leave your beggar-prince and come with me. The stupid man let his stepmother

diddle him out of a kingdom. How can you live with a fool like that? Come with me and in Lanka you will live like a goddess.' He held out his hand and Sita shrank back against the wall of the hut. 'Come! Leave that beggar to his fate,' Ravana said scornfully. 'You're worthy of better.'

The insults to Rama roused Sita's anger. 'I suppose you think that's you,' she said tartly. 'Does a puddle compare itself to the ocean? How dare you compare yourself to my lord?'

Ravana didn't care for the insults. 'I can reduce mountains to dust and whip up storms in the ocean,' he said. 'Willing or unwilling, you will come with me.'

Lunging, he scooped Sita into his arms and carried the struggling princess to his chariot. 'O Rama, Lakshmana, help me!' she cried, 'Rama where are you? He's taking me away!'

'Fly with all possible speed,' Ravana said to the driver, locking the chariot door.

As the chariot rose into the air Sita tried to leap out but Ravana held her fast. The chariot banked sharply and flew off south. Sita, weeping hopelessly, gazed at the sea of trees that lay far below. 'Oh you champa trees with your golden blooms, tell my husband where I am. Tell him that I did not leave, that Ravana has taken me away by force. Tell him that the coward waited till I was alone and helpless. Oh Godavari winding through the flame trees, carry my teardrops that fall on your bosom to my Rama. Tell him my eyes will not dry till they see him again.'

eaten some sweets,

The wise minister

• *Illustrated by Rajit Banerjee* •

There once lived a king who had a wise and clever minister called Chatura. He seemed to know everything and the king came to the conclusion that Chatura could read minds. Chatura protested that he couldn't, that he only observed things, but the king refused to believe him and so they quarrelled.

'Everyone says you can read minds and you won't even show me how you do it,' the king said angrily.

'I truly cannot read minds, sire,' Chatura said quietly.

'I don't believe what he says; I'll trick him into proving he can,' thought the king, giving Chatura a sly look. 'Let's go riding,' he said to him.

Chatura and the king rode into the nearby forest and came across a man.

'Chatura, do you see that man there?' asked the king.

'Yes, sire,' said Chatura.

'What do you think he does for a living?' he asked.

'He is a carpenter, your majesty,' Chatura replied without hesitation.

'And what is his name?' the king asked craftily.

'The same as mine, Chatura,' said the minister.

The king gave him a sharp look and said, 'Give him some money. He looks hungry and in need of food.'

'That's not necessary, sire,' said Chatura, 'he's not hungry. He's just eaten some sweets.'

'You appear to know a lot about a total stranger,' the king said stonily. 'Now let's ask him and see if you are right.' 'Of course he is,' the king thought peevishly, 'he can read minds.'

They rode up to the man. 'Are you a carpenter named Chatura, and have you just eaten some sweets?' asked the king.

The man looked up in surprise. 'Yes I am, and yes I've just eaten some sweets. But how do you know that?'

'Never mind,' said the king, glaring at his minister.

When they returned to the palace, the king sent for all his ministers and courtiers and told them how Chatura knew so much about a total stranger. 'And you still say you can't read minds!' snapped the king looking at Chatura.

'I cannot read minds, sire,' Chatura insisted without heat. 'All I did was make sense of what I saw. I knew the man's name because when you said my name, he turned around. I knew he was a carpenter from the way he was checking the trees, chipping off bits to see if the wood was hard. As for the sweets, there were some flies buzzing around his mouth.'

The king began to smile and then shouted with laughter. 'You've not only shown me you don't read minds, but also that I don't understand what my eyes see! For we both saw the same things!'

Chatura sighed with relief. Being around an angry king is very uncomfortable.

earth!' Uruvashi, instead of feeling sad, was overjoyed.

Uruvashi and Pururavasa

• *Illustrated by Sonali Biswas* •

Uruvashi, the celestial nymph, was the loveliest woman in heaven, lovelier even than the apsaras who came out of the foaming ocean. This is her story.

Once the great ascetic sage gods—Nara and Narayana—were immersed in deep meditation and Indra grew afraid they would depose him, so great were the powers they had accumulated. He thought to break their penance by sending the alluring ocean-born apsaras to their hermitage in Badarika. The ravishing apsaras began to dance and sing in front of the mighty sages and they opened their eyes. Wordlessly they gazed at the heartbreakingly beautiful maidens who sang as sweetly as the mountain thrush. Then their anger rose and Narayana, eyes snapping with rage, thought 'Indra!' and the god appeared, hesitant and wary.

'So you think to break our penance with beautiful damsels! Here,' he said slapping his thigh, 'I will give you beauty!'

A tendril of smoke rose from the thigh and from it a maiden emerged, so very beautiful that the god gasped. From her dark curling hair to her dainty feet, she was beauty personified. '*This* is beauty,' Narayana said scathingly, 'and even a woman such as this cannot disturb our piety. And you thought to do that with your apsaras?! Take her—I give her to you so that each time you look at her you will remember your stupidity. She is Uruvashi, because she sprang from my uru, my thigh.'

A shamefaced Indra bowed to the mighty sages and returned to heaven with Uruvashi. The gods fought over her and vied for her favours but she would have none of them. Then she heard of Indra's friend, the dashing, handsome King Pururavasa and she was filled with a strange longing.

Then came a time when Brahma cursed her, 'You will leave heaven and go to earth!' Uruvashi, instead of feeling sad, was overjoyed. Now she could go and see this king whose very name made her heart flutter like a turtle-dove. 'I wonder if he is as handsome as they say he is,' she thought as she went down to earth.

Cloaking herself with invisibility, Uruvashi went to Pururavasa's capital. She found him in the garden, sitting under a fragrant champa tree. 'Ah! He is even more

handsome than Kama,' she thought. For a while she stood there, too shy to reveal herself. 'He will think I am brash and bold, shameless, coming here without an invitation.' Then scolding herself for being foolish, she removed the invisibility and stood before him in all her glory.

Pururavasa stared at her and knew he would never see such loveliness again. It was all in her. Their locked gazes mirrored their love and longing.

'Ah! Uruvashi, now that you're on earth, marry me,' the king proposed ardently.

'I will,' Uruvashi said softly, 'but I have three conditions. One, I have two lambs with me. Never must any harm come to them. Two, I eat only ghee; you must never force me to eat anything else. ~~And last, I must never see you without your clothes.~~ Break any one and I'll be gone.'

Uruvashi and Pururavasa were married and lived in great happiness for many years and the passing days only increased their love.

In heaven, however, things were not well. The gods missed their lovely Uruvashi. She was not the best singer or dancer, yet all the recitals were flat without her. The plays were dull as tarnished copper for, as an actress, Uruvashi had no peer. And now, though her term of exile was over, there was still no sign of her.

'Where has she hidden herself?' Indra wondered. He sent for his divine musicians, the Gandharvas. 'Send out search parties to the four corners of the earth. Find Uruvashi,' he commanded, 'and bring her back.'

The Gandharvas flew off and one group found her in Pururavasa's palace. She looked so happy that they knew she wouldn't return to heaven just for the asking. Invisible, they roamed at will through the palace, listening to gossip. And that is how they found out about Uruvashi's three conditions. 'Ha! We'll have her back in heaven before the night is out,' said one. 'Some of us must steal the lambs while others make sure Uruvashi sees the king minus his robes!'

Late in the night, when the palace lay in darkness, a few Gandharvas sneaked into the pen and stole the lambs. The animals bleated and baa-ed as the laughing musicians flew off with them.

Uruvashi, sleeping with the king, heard the cries and shook her husband awake. 'Get up! My lambs—something's the matter with them. Go at once! If they are harmed in any way I'll leave you,' she cried, angry, and afraid for her pets.

Pururavasa jumped out of bed, grabbed his sword and without stopping to dress ran towards the door. When he was halfway across the chamber the Gandharvas released a bolt of Indra's lightning and, in the blinding purple-white light, Uruvashi saw her husband, ~~naked as the day he was born.~~

The Gandharvas laughed merrily when they saw Uruvashi's furious face. 'This should bring her back!' they chortled.

Returning to heaven, they told the gods how they had tricked the king. 'Uruvashi will be here very soon.'

Pururavasa chased the Gandharvas who had flown off with the lambs and soon caught up with them. To his surprise they returned the creatures without a fight, eyes brimming with suppressed laughter. He quickly returned to the palace and found Uruvashi dressed in her cloud-like draperies and celestial jewels. Taking the lambs from him she said coldly, 'You've broken the pact, I saw you without your clothes on so I am returning to heaven.'

'Don't leave,' the king pleaded. 'I didn't dress because you were frantic about your pets.'

'That changes nothing and I must leave,' Uruvashi said and vanished.

Pururavasa was heartbroken. He left the kingdom and wandered all over the land in search of his beloved. When he reached the great plain of Kurukshetra he saw Uruvashi there. He begged her to return to him but Uruvashi said that was impossible. 'Return to your kingdom and rule,' she advised. 'Forget all about me.'

'That's the one thing I cannot do,' the unhappy king said. 'I'll stay here and pray to Vishnu until he sends you back to me.'

Pururavasa stayed at that spot for years, out in the rain and scorching heat, praying to Vishnu. After sixty years, Vishnu, pleased by his devotion, said to Indra, 'Have the Gandharvas take Uruvashi back to Pururavasa.'

Uruvashi returned to the king and lived with him till his days on earth came to an end.

The princes get a guru

• Illustrated by Neeta Gangopadhya •

Bhishma, the patriarch of the Kurus, noticed the growing animosity between the cousins. 'These wild colts need some bridling. Their energy must be put to some constructive good,' he thought, when his spies brought him the news of Duryodhana's attempt on Bhima's life. 'They need another guru, Acharya Kripa is too gentle.'

Bhishma sent out his scouts but none of the sages proved satisfactory. The guru for his grandsons had to be an expert in warfare and weapons, in statecraft and morality. And he had to have enough presence to command the respect of the princes. So the search went on.

One day the princes were playing with a ball in a field outside the palace. The ball fell into a dry well and the boys milled around the rim, wondering how they could get it out. As wild ideas went back and forth, they heard a mocking laugh behind them. Turning around they saw a wiry, dark brahmin, leaning against a tree.

'So much for your kshatriya skills,' the man said with light mockery, 'some warriors you will make—can't even get a ball out of a well!'

The tone jarred on the princes. 'Can you?' they asked bristling.

In reply the brahmin took off a ring from his finger and threw it into the well. 'I'll fetch both the ring and the ball,' he said.

The princes laughed rudely. 'You're just a brahmin! You're bragging!'

'Am I?' the man asked and, bending, plucked some long stiff stalks of grass. Holding them in his hands, he whispered a mantra and the stalks hardened into small sharp spears. Going to the edge of the well he threw one in with such force, it embedded

itself into the ball. Blades were hurled in quick succession, each one piercing the other until a chain was formed and, effortlessly, the brahmin drew the ball up. Placing it next to him he unslung his bow and shot an arrow into the well with mind-boggling speed. The arrow tore down, and bouncing off the rock on which the ring lay flew up with the ornament on the arrow-head. The man caught the arrow as it emerged and slipped the ring on his finger. He turned to the princes and with a bow that was more rude than respectful, held the ball out to the boys.

The princes stood gaping like sheep. Then with folded palms they bowed deeply. 'Who are you, sir?' they asked respectfully. 'We've never seen anyone shoot like that.'

The brahmin smiled at the awestruck boys. 'Doesn't matter who I am. Just go tell your grandfather Bhishma what you just saw.'

Before the princes could say anything the brahmin strode away.

The princes ran back to the palace and charged into Bhishma's chamber.

'What is all the excitement about?' he asked with a fond smile.

A dozen voices broke out. 'One of you please,' said the patriarch patiently. The babble died down. 'There was this man, a brahmin. He handled the bow like a wizard! Got our ball and his ring out of the well,' Yudhishthira said.

As the tale unfolded, a broad smile lit the strong old face. 'This can only be Drona,' Bhishma said softly.

Dismissing the boys, he summoned a guard. 'Go find out if Acharya Kripa's brother-in-law is visiting him.'

'He is, your honour,' the guard informed him when he returned.

Bhishma's long strides quickly took him across the palace-grounds to Kripa's house. When he entered he saw Drona sitting with Kripa.

The two old friends embraced each other. 'I knew it was you,' Bhishma said. 'No other archer could have done that.'

'And I knew their story would bring you here,' Drona said with a laugh.

'You have come as an answer to my prayer,' Bhishma said, getting serious. 'We both studied under the same guru but I can't teach the boys—the cares of the kingdom take all my time. Yet I want the best for the boys and the best means you. Will you be the guru of the Kuru princes?' he asked.

'Yes, I will,' Drona said, 'but they will not live in the palace, they will live with me and do as I bid.'

'They most definitely will,' Bhishma assured him. 'It is still the custom.'

Drona become the princes' guru, and for the next few years he kept them hard at work leaving them no time for serious enmity.

The burning of Lanka

• Illustrated by Avishek Sen •

Rama killed Maricha and watched as the lovely golden deer turned into an old demon as it died. 'No deer for my Sita now,' he thought as he walked back to the hermitage. On the way he met Lakshmana. 'What are you doing here? Didn't I tell you to stay with Sita?' Rama asked, surprised to find his brother had disobeyed him.

'Maricha called out for help in your voice and she thought it was you,' Lakshmana said heavily. 'I told her it wasn't, that you would never screech for help, but there was no reasoning with her. When I refused to leave her, she said some very ugly things, and so here I am,' Lakshmana explained unhappily.

'She must have been overwrought. How could you have taken her seriously?' Rama asked.

They returned to the hermitage as quickly as they could and found it empty. There was no sign of Sita. They searched for her everywhere—in the kadam grove, on the banks of the Godavari, near the lotus pond, but they couldn't find Sita.

Tired, depressed, sad and angry, Rama sat down outside the hermitage holding his head in his hands. 'I am not going to return to Ayodhya. You go back when the exile's over and rule. I don't want anything. I am going to stay right here, where I spent my last happy days with Sita.'

Lakshmana said nothing for he was even more unhappy than Rama. He blamed himself for leaving Sita alone. Sita's pet deer gathered around Rama and one kept tugging at his clothes. A flicker of hope shone in Rama's eyes. 'Look, Lakshmana! I think Sita's deer is asking me to follow it,' he said rising.

The brothers followed the deer and they hadn't gone far when Rama found a chaplet of flowers on the ground. 'Just this morning, I tied these flowers in Sita's hair. Why are they lying here?' But Lakshmana had no answer and they walked on in silence.

For days they walked, following the deer which went due south. Rama was almost giving up hope of finding his beloved wife when they came upon a gigantic vulture, lying in his own blood. Feebly it called out to Rama. 'Prince of Ayodhya, come close, I have little time left. Ravana, King of Lanka, has your wife. They flew over this forest and I saw Sita crying and struggling as I was circling above. I attacked Ravana but I was no match for him. I stayed alive only to tell you what I know,' the vulture said and breathed his last.

Now Rama knew who had kidnapped Sita and where she was, but he had no army and, even if he did, how would he cross the great ocean to reach the island kingdom of Lanka. The brothers followed Sita's trail and met many strange and wondrous beings. One of them advised Rama to get the help of Sugriva, King of the Vanaras, giant ape-like men with superhuman powers. Rama met Sugriva and agreed to help him regain his kingdom. In return he promised to help Rama get Sita back. Sugriva's greatest and most trusted friend was Hanuman, the most powerful of all the Vanaras. He gave Rama a little cloth-bundle. When Rama opened it he saw Sita's jewels and wept. 'How did you get this?' he asked.

'A chariot flew over this hill and a pale, sad-eyed lady dropped it,' said Hanuman.

'I'll find you, Sita,' Rama swore softly. 'That I promise.'

Rama helped Sugriva get his kingdom back and when the rainy season was over Sugriva sent search parties in all directions to look for Sita. Hanuman's party went south, to the blue ocean's edge. There he met the brother of the old vulture who had tried to save Sita. He told Hanuman that Ravana had taken Sita to Lanka. 'Lanka is a hundred miles away, in the middle of the ocean. It is the most glorious city on earth. Maya, the architect of the gods, built the city himself. One of you mighty Vanaras can surely cross the ocean and rescue the poor princess.'

The others in the group decided that Hanuman was the only one amongst them who could fly across the ocean. 'You are the son of Vayu, god of the wind, if anyone can make it across you can. We'll wait here for you.'

Hanuman climbed a nearby hill and took off from the peak. Above him lay the blue sky and beneath lay the blue ocean. When he was halfway across, Mainaka, the mountain that hides in the ocean, poked its mighty head out. 'Rest on me for a while, hero. You are mighty indeed to fly out so far.'

'Thank you, but I can't stop now,' Hanuman called as he whizzed past.

When he approached the shores of Lanka, Surasa, the mother of all serpents, raised her massive, hideous head, blocking Hanuman's path. 'You can't go on unless you enter my mouth and if you get in, you'll never get out,' she cackled and opened her mouth. The upper jaw touched the sky and the lower lay beneath the crested waves.

Hanuman sighed. 'I've really no time for games, serpent mother, but I suppose I'll have to play.' In the blink of an eye he became as tiny as a fly and flew into her mouth and out before she could snap her jaws shut. As he emerged he grew back to his own impressive size and laughed into her surprised face. 'I've done as you asked, now please step aside. I really must be on my way.'

Surasa blessed him and disappeared into the deep blue depths. Hanuman flew over the white sandy shore and the dark green forest till he came to a small range of hills. There, gleaming on the highest peak, lay the city of Lanka.

Hanuman gazed down in wonder at the marble towers that rose into the sky and the quartz turrets shining like huge gems. Then, making himself as small as a cat, he landed outside the city walls. Returning to his normal size he walked up to the city gates, killed the guards and went in. He walked down the broad streets lined with beautiful trees and into a great parkland.

'How will I find the princess in this great big city,' he thought. 'Maybe the king's palace is where I should go. The gossips there will be talking of nothing else but Sita.'

Turning himself the size of a mouse, Hanuman sneaked into the palace and wandered everywhere, from the court to the kitchens. And it wasn't long before he learnt that Sita was in the Ashoka garden. When the city fell asleep, Hanuman went to the fabled garden and saw a lovely little palace. It was made of pure white marble and the slender pillars were delicately carved and inlaid with gold and precious gems. It stood twinkling in the moonlight like something out of a dream. Hanuman peeped into the rooms but they were all empty. Scratching his head he looked around when he heard someone weeping. The sound came from a small thatched hut. He went closer. 'Oh why did I send Lakshmana away?' he heard a voice say. 'It's my fault I am

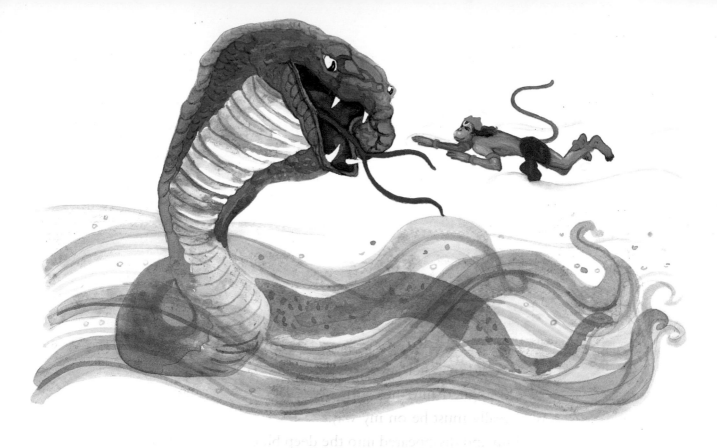

in this mess. How will my lord find me? I am alive only because my eyes want to see him again.'

Hanuman peered into the window and saw a frail lady with long dishevelled hair hunched in a corner. Her clothes were in tatters and not a jewel graced her arm or neck. But her face was delicately moulded and so very beautiful. 'This is the princess,' Hanuman breathed. 'Fool that I was to look for her in the palace. I should have known she would have spurned Ravana's wealth.'

Quickly climbing a tree just outside the hut, he turned himself into a small monkey and said, 'Princess of Ayodhya, look up, I have crossed the ocean for Rama, to find you.'

Sita's ceaseless tears stopped flowing when she heard Rama's name. 'Who talks to me?' she said getting up and looking around. The only thing she could see was a little monkey in the tree. 'Take heart, you will soon be rescued,' the little creature said.

'Has Rama sent you? Oh, how is my lord?' she asked as tears ran down her cheeks.

'Pining for you, but now all will be well,' Hanuman said comfortingly.

'Is he here, in Lanka?' Sita whispered.

'No, but he will be,' Hanuman assured the unhappy princess.

'If he doesn't come in the next couple of months, Ravana plans to marry me by force. He comes here everyday and begs me to marry him. Now he's running out of patience,' Sita told him.

'Rama will be here long before that,' Hanuman said bracingly. 'Don't worry, princess. Now, with your permission, I must leave.'

'When you see my lord tell him I live only to see him again,' Sita said as he left the grove.

Hanuman scouted the army quarters to find out the military strength of Lanka and checked the walls of the fort for weak points. 'One should know one's enemy well so I must do something that will take me to Ravana's presence.' He quickly returned to the grove and, growing back to his normal size, began uprooting trees, ripping the vines and scattering the flowers. 'This should do the trick,' he thought, grinning wickedly.

News reached Ravana that a monkey was creating havoc in his garden. Ravana burst into laughter. 'How much harm can a monkey do? Guards, go scare that monkey away,' he said.

A small group of soldiers went into the garden but Hanuman, growing taller than the palace towers, killed the lot. Ravana then sent a whole battalion but Hanuman, thoroughly angry, flattened the

soldiers with a huge iron club. Finally Ravana sent his son Indrajit to capture the mighty Vanara. Indrajit shot Hanuman with a flaming arrow. Screaming with pain, Hanuman flew up into the sky. To his surprise, so did the prince. The two fought long and hard and at last Indrajit struck Hanuman with Brahma's weapon and the mighty hero fell to the ground and lay still. Indrajit's soldiers bound him in chains. 'Stop!' the prince cried as he stepped on the ground, 'the chains will nullify the effects of the Brahma missile!'

But he was too late. Hanuman rose, flexed his powerful muscles, rattled the chains and said to his captors, 'Lead on.'

The soldiers, who had expected him to break the chains, meekly led him into Ravana's presence.

Ravana sat on his high throne flanked by his councillors and Hanuman looked at him in genuine admiration and regret. 'What a fine specimen of manhood. And he's reputed to have a fine mind. A great pity it's used to do evil.'

Ravana was just as impressed by Hanuman. 'Who are you?' he asked. 'And why have you destroyed my garden and killed my men?'

'I am Hanuman, a Vanara, and I uprooted those trees because I knew it would lead me to you. And just so you know, I am in these chains only because I choose to be. I came here to find the Princess of Ayodhya and I've done that. If I were you I would quickly restore her to her lord,' he said conversationally, 'otherwise you and your kingdom will be destroyed.'

Ravana rose, blazing with anger. 'Put him to death!' he snarled. 'How dare you tell me what to do?!'

'You can't kill an envoy,' Ravana's brother said quietly. 'Keep your anger for his master, the Prince of Ayodhya.'

'All right, if you insist,' Ravana said with a nasty smile. 'But I want this monkey's tail cut off! He'll be a joke without it. Now wrap it up in oil-soaked rags, set it alight and parade him in the streets of Lanka. Let the people see how we treat a spy!'

Hanuman smiled grimly. This stupid king was going to show him the whole city, the arsenal, the entry points and where it could be breached. He allowed the guards to bind his tail and lead him out into the city. A huge mob followed crying, 'Kill him! Kill him!' and children pelted him with stones.

Women poured out of their homes bearing pots of oil which they emptied on to the rags that bound his tail. When the tail was set alight the mob cheered. Hanuman, the pure-hearted, did not feel the heat or pain and walked through the city noting everything. After he had seen all he wanted he shrank to the size of a mouse and the chains fell in a heap to the ground. 'Now I'll teach these Lankan rakshasas a lesson they will not forget.'

Before the astonished soldiers could react, he leapt onto a roof, becoming enormous once more. Weaving his blazing tail, Hanuman leapt from rooftop to rooftop setting the mansions and palaces on fire. First one street blazed and then another and soon the whole city was on fire. Panic-stricken people ran screaming with nowhere to go. Some brave ones hurled pots and pans and knives and stones at the Vanara who just laughed at their antics. Then a great wind came in from the ocean and fanned the flames which rose higher and higher. The billowing black smoke turned day into night. As Hanuman leapt onto the roof of Ravana's palace, he stopped in mid-flight, slapping himself on the forehead. 'Oh what a fool I am! The princess will be burnt to death if I set the king's palace on fire.' A few mighty bounds and he was in the Ashoka garden. He sighed with relief when he saw Sita standing outside her hut watching the red-gold flames that lit the sky.

He went up to her and bowed. 'Be brave princess, before you know it Rama will be here with an army of Vanaras to rescue you.' Then leaping into the air he flew north across the ocean, to the hilltop where Rama and Lakshmana were waiting eagerly for news of Sita.

A friend in need

• *Illustrated by Sujata Bansal* •

A fox made its den near a pond and his best friend was a tortoise. One day when the two were sitting chatting idly, a leopard came to the pond for a drink.

The fox leapt up like a scalded cat. 'Watch out!' he cried to the tortoise as he dashed into his den.

But his poor friend couldn't move fast enough and the leopard caught him. As the leopard's paw fell on him, the tortoise quickly retreated into his shell. The leopard tried to bite into the shell but could not. His fangs couldn't even make a dent. He tried raking it with his claws but there was not a scratch on the shell.

The fox who was anxiously watching his friend called out, 'Sir, leopard, if you want to crack the shell you must soften it. Just throw it into the pond and when the shell soaks up enough water you'll be able to break it open and have a good meal.'

'Brilliant idea!' said the stupid leopard throwing the tortoise into the pond.

The grateful tortoise called out a hasty 'thank you' as he dived into the murky green waters. And the grinning fox retired into his burrow and left the leopard gnashing his fangs in anger.

Shiva and Sati

• Illustrated by Suddhasattwa Basu •

Brahma, the Creator, was extremely worried. The Great God Shiva was an ascetic and would not wed. But wed he must, Brahma decided, for without him creation would come to naught.

'Something must be done,' Brahma said to Vishnu.

Vishnu pondered on the problem and found a solution. 'We must ask Uma to be born as Daksha's daughter, Sati, and her purpose must be to win Shiva's love. Only she can do that.'

The goddess agreed to the proposal and was born as Daksha's daughter.

Daksha, the First Father, son of Brahma, born from his right thumb, was proud and arrogant and a stickler for propriety. He had great plans for Sati, his ravishingly beautiful daughter, but there was only one thing about her he didn't like—her unwavering devotion to that unkempt Shiva. 'Goodness knows what she sees in him,' he thought in exasperation.

One day Brahma and his son Narada came to Daksha's palace.

'Sati, my child, pay your respects to your grandfather,' Daksha said.

Sati knelt before the Creator with folded palms and Brahma pronounced a blessing which made her father scowl. 'May Shiva, the auspicious one, be your husband. The bright god has never taken a consort and will never take another. But I warn you, you won't find it easy to win him,' he added.

Sati's heart leapt like a fawn in spring. 'There's nothing I won't do to win him,' she thought. 'I will immerse myself in penance and meditation, prove to him that I too can live like an ascetic.'

Sati left the palace and went into the forest, much to her father's disgust. There she sat and meditated on the god whose only ornament was the crescent moon on his brow. She sat there for years, caring nothing for the burning sun or the icy wind, rain, hail, sleet or snow. The seasons were all the same to her, as was hunger and thirst, so completely did she forget herself.

The gods rejoiced when they saw her absolute devotion. 'It's time now to go to Shiva,' Brahma said to Vishnu.

The gods went to Kailasha, disturbing the serenity in Shiva's mountain fastness. Shiva opened his eyes and smiled when he saw the host of assembled gods with Brahma and Vishnu in the lead. 'To what do I owe this honour?' he asked, faintly mocking.

'It is time you took a wife, Shiva, just as Vishnu and I have. You know it is vital to creation,' said Brahma.

A singularly sweet smile softened the handsome but austere face of the ascetic god. 'All right, I will marry, provided you can find me a woman who will do yoga with me at my level and also be a wife to me.'

'My granddaughter can meet your conditions,' Brahma said, unable to hide his triumph.

Shiva's sceptical look made Vishnu smile. 'Sati, Daksha's daughter, does fit the bill,' Vishnu told him. 'At the moment she's immersed in penances that even you would consider noteworthy.'

'I'll go have a look,' was all Shiva could promise.

Shiva went to the forest where Sati was meditating and the Great God was visibly impressed. Sati sat immobile, her frail, slender form ravaged by the seasons, and yet there was a radiance in her face that was brighter than the crescent moon on his brow. The ascetic god was ensnared and Kama, the god of love, congratulated himself. This was his greatest catch!

'You please me greatly, daughter of Daksha,' Shiva said. 'Ask for a boon.'

Sati's eyes flew open and her whole being filled with happiness. 'Lord…I…want you for my husband,' came the halting plea.

'It shall be so,' said Shiva with a broad smile.

Shiva returned to Kailasha and thought of Brahma, who appeared. 'I'll marry Sati but you had better tell your son Daksha about it. He, for some reason, dislikes me intensely. I think part of the problem is my sense of style, he thinks I've none,' Shiva said with a careless laugh.

Brahma went to Daksha and told him Shiva was willing to marry his daughter Sati. Daksha was livid. 'How dare Shiva presume he's good enough for my daughter! I'll never let Sati marry that ash-smeared mendicant,' he almost shouted, but one doesn't shout at the Creator.

'Your feelings do not matter,' Brahma stated coldly. 'It must be so.'

And so, much against his wishes, Daksha made preparations for his daughter's wedding. All the gods attended and after the ceremony, Shiva took Sati to Kailasha. Sometime later, some aeons to be precise, there was a great sacrifice which was attended by all the gods and divine beings. When Daksha entered the hall the gods rose, all except Brahma and Shiva that is.

Daksha was furious when Shiva did not get up to greet him. 'You should rise when I enter, like the other gods!' Daksha fumed, adding pompously, 'I am your father-in-law and the First Father of all mankind.'

Shiva knew better than to explain that if he, Shiva, rose, it would be Daksha who would be the loser for, whatever Daksha thought, Shiva outranked all the gods. Shiva remained seated, a faint smile on his lips and Daksha's rage boiled over. 'You uncivilized boor! I never wanted my daughter to marry you! Just look at you, you don't wear proper clothes, wind snakes around your neck and I doubt your hair has ever felt a comb! I should never have let Brahma persuade me.'

When Shiva still refused to rise Daksha stormed out. He went home and made preparations for a mighty sacrifice that would last a thousand years. All the gods and goddesses were invited except Shiva and Sati. When Sati heard about it, she was hurt and offended but Shiva was absolutely unaffected by the deliberate snub.

'Let's go to my father's palace,' Sati said to him, 'I wish to attend this great ceremony.'

'But my dear, we haven't been invited,' Shiva pointed out, laughing into her lovely, angry face.

'But I want to go,' Sati insisted. 'Why shouldn't I go to my father's house?'

'Very well, my dear, you shall go, but no good will come of this,' Shiva said quietly. 'Nandi and my ganas will escort you but I'll give it a miss. Your father will much prefer that.'

Sati went to her father's palace riding on Nandi and followed by thousands of Shiva's attendants. When she entered the great hall Daksha rudely turned his face away, but Sati went forward and dutifully touched her parents' feet. As ghee was poured into the sacred flames, Sati's sense of injury mounted. 'Why were my husband and I not invited?' she asked her father in cool, clear tones. Then turning to Brahma and Vishnu she said, 'How could you condone this insult to my lord?'

'That's enough Sati!' Daksha snapped. 'I didn't invite your husband because he isn't fit for company. He is a barbarian, wanders around in cemeteries, worshipped by the imps and demons of the night, and cares nothing about the offering he gets—is satisfied with just a bel leaf,' he said scornfully.

Sati's eyes smouldered but her father didn't heed the warning signs. With unequalled stupidity he added, 'Anyhow, now that you're here, sit down and partake of these sacrificial offerings.'

Sati froze, for a moment speechless with rage. Then she rounded on her father. 'How dare you slight my lord in front of all the gods! He doesn't need the trappings of divinity you find so essential, he is above all that. You forget, of all the gods, including Brahma and Vishnu, only my lord is Mahadeva—the Great God. I am ashamed to call myself your daughter. I will rid myself of this body right here and now!' A heavy stillness fell in the hall and even the sacred fire grew silent. 'May flames consume this worthless body!' she cried out. 'My lord, I'll return to you when I have a father I can respect and who respects you.'

Great orange gold flames sprang up around Sati and when they died out all that remained was a small heap of ashes.

Cries of horror rang in the hall as the stupefied gods found their voices. 'Alas! Sati is dead! Shiva's beloved lives no more! Daksha will pay dearly.'

Nandi and the ganas who were waiting outside charged in when they heard the cries. 'Kill Daksha! Don't spare him,' cried Nandi but the gods came to Daksha's rescue and Nandi and the ganas were forced to flee. They returned to Kailasha and told Shiva all that had happened. The world shuddered when Shiva rose raging in anguish and grief. He tore out a lock of his hair hurling it on the ground and a terrible being rose and bowed before Shiva. 'Kill Daksha!' Shiva thundered, 'and all who stand in your way.'

The mighty demon flew to Daksha's palace, slaughtered Daksha's men and then beheaded Daksha. Brahma looked at his son's body sadly and said, 'Daksha must live again and his sacrifice must be completed.'

Vishnu sighed. 'Only Shiva can restore him to life,' he said quietly.

The gods, though mortally afraid, went to Kailasha but didn't dare approach Shiva. Only Vishnu had the nerve to address him, 'Be merciful, Shiva,' he said. 'Give Daksha life and let him complete the sacrifice for the benefit of all creation.'

Shiva, never one for extracting his pound of flesh, agreed and went to the great hall. 'Bring me the head of the sacrificial goat,' he said. 'I will give him life but he will never forget his place in the scheme of things.' Shiva joined the goat's head to Daksha's neck and Daksha rose as if from a deep sleep. Now stripped of all his pride and vanity, he knelt before Shiva and begged forgiveness. Then he rose and the flames of the sacred fire crackled once more.

The sacrifice complete, Shiva got up to leave when he saw Sati's body on the platform. Even the gods didn't know how it came to be there and they sat rooted with fear.

A devastating grief, deeper and vaster than the ocean, engulfed Shiva as he stooped and picked up the body of his beloved. An agonizing cry tore out of his lips and, clutching the body, he ran into the mountains. His demented cries woke up sleeping volcanoes, caused rivers to tear out their banks, and mountain peaks to totter and explode. The gods knew that if Shiva grieved much longer all creation would be destroyed. They had to stop his grieving but Shiva would grieve as long as he held Sati's body. Then Vishnu had an idea. 'We must rid him of Sati's body.'

As Shiva wandered across the mountains, Vishnu followed the sorrowing god and, without Shiva noticing, he cut off bits of the body until nothing remained. Only then did Shiva's grief abate and sanity return to the god of destruction. The gods breathed a great sigh of profound relief—the world had been inches away from destruction. They knew that many ages would pass before they could demand that he wed again. But the gods have all the time in the world.

Shiva returned to Kailasha, joyless and remote. He plunged himself into a trance-like meditation, and for aeons he remained aloof from the worlds of gods and men. Ages would pass before Sati would return as Parvati, daughter of Himavat, lord of the towering Himalayas, and marry her Shiva once again.

The holy parrot

• Illustrated by Atanu Roy •

Birbal's intelligence and wit were not used only to solve his Emperor's problems. Anyone in trouble could apply to him and would be certain to get help.

One morning the Emperor's personal attendant came running to him in tears.

'What's the matter?' Birbal asked the old man.

'O huzur—that parrot—it's dead!' he wailed.

'Why should a dead parrot reduce you to tears?' Birbal asked the flustered man.

'O huzur, this is a special parrot, a holy fakir gave it to the Emperor!' the old man wept.

'So it's a special parrot, but why these tears?' Birbal asked with a smile.

'It's not the stupid parrot I am crying for, it's for me,' the old man said wiping his eyes with the edge of his unravelling turban. 'Some months ago the Emperor handed me a parrot and said, "Look after this bird well—a great pir gave it to me. And if anyone brings me news of its death, I'll have him beheaded!" And now it's dead and I can't go and tell the Emperor that, he'll have my head!'

Birbal patted the frightened man's shoulder. 'Don't worry, old one, I'll tell the Emperor.'

'Then he'll take your head!' the old man cried.

'No, he won't,' Birbal said laughing. 'Go back and leave it to me.'

The old man grabbed Birbal's hand and kissed it. 'Thank you,

huzur, thank you,' he said fervently.

Birbal found the Emperor in court discussing serious matters with sages of all faiths. Akbar smiled when he saw him. 'Ah Birbal! What are you doing here? Weren't you planning to go out of the city for a while?' he asked.

'I was, sire, but I didn't because I have some very important news for you. Do you remember the parrot the pir gave you?' he asked. Emperors easily forget such things.

'Certainly I do,' the Emperor said.

'I just went to see it and I must say it is a very holy bird indeed,' Birbal said.

'Nonsense, Birbal,' the Emperor remarked, a little testy, 'one doesn't call birds "holy".'

'Well this parrot certainly appears to be. It was lying on its back, face to the sky, eyes closed, deep in meditation,' said Birbal.

'Is this some kind of a joke, Birbal?' the Emperor asked coldly.

'No, your majesty, I am in earnest,' Birbal answered.

'This I must see,' the Emperor said rising.

Akbar, followed by trailing courtiers, went to see the holy parrot. He took one look at the bird and turned to Birbal, 'That is not a holy bird, it is a dead bird,' he said, his voice rising in anger.

The courtiers grew still and wary. Everyone does when faced with angry emperors; only Birbal showed no sign of fear.

'So it is, sire,' he said serenely.

'Then what was all that rubbish about the "holy" bird?' the Emperor asked, a little puzzled.

'A little matter of keeping my head on my neck, sire,' Birbal smiled.

For a moment the Emperor was baffled and then it dawned on him. 'Ah! So this is how you give me news of its death, by not giving it to me!' he said laughing. 'And you saved an old man's life. I am glad I have you, for you, Birbal, are worth a hundred wise men!'

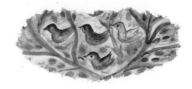

The eye and the bird

• Illustrated by Ludmilla Chakrabarty •

Drona was a stern teacher, tough on discipline. The princes had to master archery, fighting with a mace, fighting from chariot, horseback or elephant, and the secrets of the sword. Soon even the clumsiest prince showed signs of promise. Some excelled in one field, some in two, some in more, but his star pupil was Arjuna. He was an all-rounder and could use the bow almost with Shiva's skill, and to crown it all he was ambidextrous. He could shoot with both hands equally well and was the only one with bowstring scars on both shoulders.

One morning Drona asked the princes to assemble in the target ranges. The boys rushed to obey. Their guru did not like to be kept waiting.

'Line up before that tree in the east field. I hope your bows and arrows are in order—nocks, fletches, bowstrings.'

There was a murmur of 'yes sir' as the boys fell in.

'Right then. Look up. Do you see the artificial bird in the tree?' Drona asked.

'Yes sir,' they replied.

'The aim is to sever the bird's head from the body,' Drona said. 'You will each get one chance. Yudhishthira, you first.'

The eldest Pandava positioned himself and raising his bow drew back the bowstring. But before he could release the arrow Drona asked, 'What do you see?'

'I see the tree, the leaves, the branches…'

'Back to your place!' Drona barked. 'You see nothing!'

One by one, the princes were asked to aim at the bird and each was asked the same question. All the answers were somewhat like Yudhishthira's and with every answer, Drona's anger mounted. They were variously called moron, dolt, imbecile, idiot, and the princes cringed with shame. Arjuna was the last to be called.

'You have been told the purpose of this exercise. Raise your bow,' Drona snapped.

As Arjuna drew back the bowstring, he was asked witheringly, 'What do you see?'

'The bird's head,' Arjuna said, eye on the target.

'What else? Your brothers perhaps, the tree, the sky, me?' Drona asked sarcastically.

'No sir, just the bird's head,' Arjuna replied.

The angry scowl disappeared and a faint smile curved Drona's lips. 'Release the arrow,' he commanded.

Before the words were out the arrow flew into the tree and the bird's head fell to the ground with a thud.

Drona's cold eyes raked the others who stood nervously shuffling their feet. 'You have learnt nothing. Where there should be brains you have chickpeas! What was your target? The bird's head! Your eyes have no business seeing anything else. Had this been war, none of you would have hit the mark. You would all be dead. Only Arjuna here,' he said looking fondly at him, 'will amount to something. Only he has learnt the most important lesson in archery—the target is all that the eye must see.'

The touch of Bhasmasura

• Illustrated by Avishek Sen •

Bhasmasura was a powerful king but that wasn't enough for him, he longed for absolute power. For though he had a mighty kingdom and great wealth, no one stood in awe of him, no one held him in respect.

'Real power is when men and gods look at me and tremble with fear,' he thought. 'I will acquire such power that the heavens will shudder at my name!'

Bhasmasura went deep into the forest and prayed to Shiva for many years. His penances were so terrible that the Great God came down from Kailasha and stood before him. 'What do you want?' Shiva asked kindly, pleased with his great devotion.

'I want power, lord—such power that if I touch anyone's head, man or god, with my right hand, he will be reduced to a heap of ashes.'

'So be it,' said Shiva.

Bhasmasura rose and looking at the god with a nasty gleam in his eyes began to laugh. 'I will begin with you!' he cried as he leapt forward to touch Shiva's head with his right hand. 'You shall be reduced to ashes.'

Shiva ran, cursing himself for not thinking before he granted this crazy asura a boon. 'Serves me right,' he thought as he fled down the mountain path, with Bhasmasura on his heels. Shiva raced over the mountains but Bhasmasura stayed close behind. The god's mind worked as furiously as his legs. 'Vishnu, help!' he thought and Vishnu was there. 'Do something,' cried Shiva as Bhasmasura gained on him.

'Don't worry,' Vishnu laughed, 'I'll take care of your ugly friend.'

'This is not funny,' Shiva scowled at the grinning Vishnu.

'It is, from where I stand. Now, get behind that peak,' Vishnu said turning into Mohini.

Racing round the bend, Bhasmasura stopped abruptly. Shiva had disappeared. 'Where are you?' he bawled. 'Hiding from me?...but I'll find you!'

Tinkling anklets and a divine perfume wafting in the cool breeze caught his attention. Turning around he saw a ravishing maiden gliding towards him on dainty little feet. Bhasmasura stared into her flawless face and forgot all about Shiva. Her glowing eyes smiled alluringly, mesmerizing him. 'Who are you and what are you doing alone on the wild mountainside?' he asked, in what he thought was a sweet, gentle tone.

The maiden flinched and then moving closer whispered huskily, 'I am Mohini and these mountains are my home.'

'Marry me and you will live in a palace worthy of you,' Bhasmasura said ardently. With her eyes on him, Mohini began to sway. 'Dance with me, match me step for step and I will marry you,' she said.

Mohini began to whirl and twirl, dancing with exquisite grace. Bhasmasura thumped and stomped around like a clumsy elephant, his arms flaying around like a broken scarecrow's. Graceless though he was, he managed to follow the steps. He would do anything to win her. Faster they moved, and faster, and then suddenly the dancing girl sank to the ground lightly as a leaf with her right hand resting gracefully on her head. Bhasmasura, imitating her exactly, gracelessly plonked down like a sack of cabbages and raising his right hand placed it on his head. The next moment where Bhasmasura sat, a small heap of ashes stirred in the breeze. Mohini got up, throwing the ashes a not-so-sweet smile and casually turned into Vishnu.

'Come on out, it is done,' he called, laughing.

Shiva emerged from behind the peak with a wry smile on his face. 'Thanks,' he said sheepishly. 'That was a close call.'

'Even if I do say so myself, the end was brilliantly executed,' Vishnu said and the two gods laughed as the ashes scattered in the wind.

Devayani and Kacha

• Illustrated by Sujata Singh •

T he devas and the asuras both had their gurus; Brahaspati was guru to the gods and Sukracharya was guru to the asuras. During the frequent wars between the devas and the asuras, the devas often fared badly. When their divine followers died in battle, they stayed dead, but the fallen asuras were brought back to life by their guru. Sukracharya was the only one who knew the art of Sanjivani—bringing the dead back to life—and the asuras took full advantage of it. Whenever the mood took them, they made war. The gods decided they must somehow acquire knowledge of the art. They went to their guru Brahaspati and said, 'Holy one, send your son Kacha to Sukracharya, tell him to do all he can to learn the secrets of Sanjivani.'

Kacha was an extremely handsome young man and a great favourite with the gods. And he was more than just a handsome face—he was kind, noble-hearted, brave and intelligent. The gods knew that, of them all, only Kacha could go to Sukracharya with a pure heart. 'He is the only one who does nothing for personal gain, so only he can go,' the gods said.

Brahaspati sent for his son. 'I want you to study under Sukracharya and learn all that he knows. Honour your guru and obey him in all things.'

'Yes, father,' Kacha said without arguing, though he didn't fancy living among the horrid asuras.

Kacha went to the great underground city of the asuras and was surprised by its beauty and magnificence. The great palaces were surrounded by lush gardens filled with fruits and flowers and songbirds. He walked through the city to a grove of beautiful trees at the edge of a forest. In the middle of the grove lay the hermitage of Sukracharya.

The mighty sage was sitting on the veranda when Kacha arrived. The young man touched his feet with reverence. 'I am Kacha, son of Brahaspati, and am here to learn from you,' he said. He neither hid his identity nor tried to worm his way in. 'Will you accept me as your disciple?'

Sukracharya knew why he had come but he liked his truthfulness. 'You are welcome, son of my learned friend,' he said. 'You will stay here and do whatever I tell you to do.'

Sukracharya had a beautiful daughter whom he loved more than life itself. 'Come in and meet my daughter Devayani. She will be glad to have a companion.'

When Devayani saw the handsome young deva, her heart fluttered like a trapped bird. 'Devayani, my dear, this is Kacha,' Sukracharya told her smiling fondly. 'He'll live with us until he completes his studies.'

Kacha studied with Sukracharya whenever his guru was in the hermitage. But when he was away in the asura king's court, Kacha spent his days with Devayani. He helped her with her chores and took the cattle into the forest to graze. There he collected flowers for her hair and the delicious fruits she was so fond of. At dusk, which many call the cow-dust hour, he returned with the cattle and Devayani was always there to greet him.

The asuras knew why Kacha was in their realm and were furious with Sukracharya for accepting him as his pupil. But they dared not make a complaint—their guru wouldn't take kindly to that. They thought if the studies took their normal course Kacha would soon learn how to bring the dead back to life. 'We must kill him before that happens,' the king said.

Time means nothing to the gods and Kacha spent nearly a thousand years with Sukracharya, but at no time did he press his guru to teach him the secret art of Sanjivani. And his guru showed no signs of doing so. But the asuras didn't know that and they made a plan to kill Kacha.

'He takes the cattle to graze in the forest,' said the king. 'Kill him there, when he is alone.'

One day when Kacha was in the forest, the asuras surrounded and killed him.

Then they chopped his body up into little pieces and fed it to a wolf.

When dusk fell, Devayani heard the cowbells and ran out. 'He's back,' she thought happily and then fear washed over her. The cows were back but there was no sign of Kacha. Weeping and sobbing, she ran to her father. 'Something has happened to Kacha, he hasn't come home!' she cried, eyes brimming with tears. 'Oh father, I don't want to live if he is dead!'

Sukracharya held his beloved daughter. 'Don't weep, my daughter. Am I not here with you?' he said wiping her eyes. 'Come, we'll go into the forest and look for him.'

They hadn't gone far when they came across Kacha's over-cloth lying in a pool of blood. Sukracharya performed Sanjivani and Kacha burst out of the wolf's stomach as fine and whole as he had ever been.

'Oh Kacha!' cried Devayani, weeping afresh. 'Any harm to you will kill me.'

Kacha touched Sukracharya's feet and they went home. For a time Devayani didn't leave Kacha's side, she knew the asuras would try to kill him again. But one day when they were sitting by the lotus pond, Devayani said, 'There are some flowers that grow at the end of the forest, I wish I could smell them again. I picked a few when I was a child and I can still remember their fragrance.'

'I'll get you some,' Kacha said and ran into the forest before Devayani could stop him. The asuras, who kept a constant watch on his movements, followed him and killed him again. This time they ground his body and threw it into the ocean.

When the moon rose and there was no sign of Kacha, Devayani knew he had been murdered by the asuras. 'Bring him back, father, please,' she wept brokenly.

'Don't cry, child. That's the one thing I cannot bear,' Sukracharya said. 'I'll bring him back.'

He performed the secret rites and Kacha stood before them, looking at himself in amazement.

'They killed me again,' he said touching his guru's feet. 'I owe my life to you.'

Sukracharya blessed him and Kacha gently brushed Devayani's tears away. 'Don't cry, I am all right now.'

The asuras gnashed their teeth in rage when they learnt that their guru had once more brought Kacha back to life.

'How can we make sure that Sukracharya doesn't give him life?' asked the king.

One particularly devious asura had an idea. 'Bzz, bzz, bzz,' he whispered and the king laughed evilly. 'A very good idea,' he said slapping his thigh.

A few days later when Kacha was in the forest with the cattle the asuras killed him for the third time. This time they burnt his body and dissolved the ashes in a goblet of wine. Then they went to Sukracharya and with oily respect said, 'We have brought you a goblet of fine red wine,' and handed him the golden cup.

Sukracharya who liked wine smiled with pleasure. 'Thank you, this is very kind.'

The asuras watched as their guru raised the goblet and drank the cool, red wine with an expression of enjoyment.

That evening when the cattle returned without Kacha, Devayani ran to her father, tears raining down her face. 'How many times must he die, father?' she wept. 'I know they have killed him.'

'Hush, stop crying, I'll bring him back,' said her father.

Sukracharya closed his eyes and realized at once that Kacha was inside his stomach. His eyes flew open. The problem was serious now. If he brought Kacha back to life, he would die. If he did not, his beloved daughter would pine and fade away. There was only one way out—he would have to teach Kacha the secrets of Sanjivani. Kacha absorbed the knowledge of Sanjivani from his guru and then Sukracharya performed the rites. As Kacha burst out of his stomach, Sukracharya fell dead. Kacha quickly performed the same rites over his guru and Sukracharya sat up. 'You are a good student, my son, for you are my son now— you came out of me,' he said, smiling at the handsome young man. Then rising, he said, 'Stay here till I return. I have something to say in court. They are fools, and I was a greater fool for drinking that wine! Henceforth no seeker of knowledge may drink wine.'

The asuras rose when they saw their guru striding angrily into court. 'You idiots! Fools! You forced my hand. Thanks to your abysmal stupidity, I had to teach Kacha the secrets of Sanjivani. Had you left him alone, he would never have learnt the secret art. You gave him what you tried so hard to keep from him. I can think of nothing stupider than that.'

Kacha stayed for a while longer and when his thousand-year apprenticeship was at an end, he made preparations to return home to heaven. He went to his guru and knelt at his feet. 'I must return to heaven now that my studies are over. Bless me father, before I go.'

Sukracharya placed a gentle hand on the bowed head. 'Live long and well. Give my regards to your respected father.'

Kacha then went to Devayani who was in the garden plucking flowers for a garland. 'I must go now,' he said plucking some blossoms and laying them in the basket. 'It's time I returned home.'

Tears welled up in Devayani's dark eyes. 'If you must, marry me and take me with you. I've loved you for so long.'

Kacha looked sadly at her. 'How can I marry you? I am your father's son now,' he said quietly. 'I am your brother, it will be a sin to marry you.'

The heartbroken girl wept angry, bitter tears. 'I curse you for this! You will never be able to use the secrets of Sanjivani, you will never return the dead to life!' she cried.

'Take your curse back, Devayani,' Kacha said, alarmed. 'This curse is unjust. You cannot curse me for doing what is right.'

But Devayani refused flatly and the normally even-tempered young man lost his temper. 'Your curse cannot stop me from teaching the secret art, so indirectly I will restore the dead to life. And I curse you, you will never wed a deva and live in Devaloka. A mortal will be your husband!'

And so it came to pass. Years later Devayani married Yayati, the mighty king of the lunar race, but not the god she had hoped to wed.

Ekalavya's guru-dakshina

• Illustrated by Suhrid Mukhopadhayay •

The Kuru princes were in their final term at the gurukul. Just before graduation, they decided to hunt in the nearby forest and test their skill with a bow. Arming themselves they went to the forest accompanied by some attendants and a dog. Suddenly, the dog raced ahead barking furiously. In the clearing stood a black-clad Nishada youth and the dog advanced towards him with threatening barks and growls. Before the wretched beast could close its mouth, the Nishada drew back his bowstring and quickly shot seven arrows into the gaping jaws keeping them wrenched apart. The dog now couldn't shut its mouth. Yelping in pain, it ran back to the princes.

The young royals looked down at the beast in stunned amazement. Whoever shot those arrows had no peer—not in archery at any rate! When Arjuna saw the dog, his face grew hard with jealous rage. 'We must find this marksman,' he said flatly, 'he's bound to be nearby.'

A brief search led them to the glade and what they

saw made them stop in their tracks. A slim forest-dweller stood in the clearing, shooting arrows unerringly into the heart of a target. Never had they seen such exquisite marksmanship. They watched him in silent admiration for a while.

'Who are you?' Arjuna asked tersely at last. 'Who's your guru?'

'I am Ekalavya, Prince of the Nishadas,' the youth replied, 'and my guru is Dronacharya.'

The name came as a shock to all. Arjuna stared at him in disbelief. Then without another word he turned and went straight back to the gurukul.

'What's the matter with him?' Bhima asked as Arjuna disappeared.

The others shrugged and it was decided they'd wait for him in the clearing.

Drona looked up in surprise when Arjuna entered his chamber. 'What are you doing here?' he asked and only then did he notice the tightly controlled anger and disappointment. 'Something bothering you?' he said evenly.

'You told me that I would be the world's greatest archer,' Arjuna said in flinty tones, 'yet today I saw a Nishada in the forest who makes me look like an amateur. And he says you're his guru. Tell me how can that be?'

Drona gave him a long searching look. 'Take me to this boy,' he said emotionlessly.

Arjuna took Drona to the edge of the clearing and Drona looked at the Nishada youth who held himself with such grace and nobility. The guru turned his expressionless gaze on Arjuna who looked back with hard cold eyes. With a faint nod, Drona entered the clearing. At the far end he saw a crude clay image of himself garlanded with wild flowers, but he made no comment.

When Ekalavya saw Drona he dropped his bow and humbly touched his feet. The clear eyes looked at him with unconditional love and devotion. But Drona's eyes revealed nothing as he looked down at the boy.

'How am I your guru?' he asked abruptly.

Ekalavya rose. 'Many years ago I came to you and asked you to be my guru but you refused because I am a forest-dweller,' he said sadly. 'But I wanted no other guru. My heart had chosen you and would not choose again. So I returned to the forest and made this clay statue of you. Every day, before I begin my practice, I pray to you and seek your guidance. I have never sought another guru.'

Drona's face grew cold and remote and once again he looked at Arjuna who said nothing. Something passed between them. Then he turned to Ekalavya. 'If I am your guru you owe me guru-dakshina. Will you pay the fee I ask?'

'Anything,' Ekalavya said softly. 'There is nothing I will not give my guru.'

'Then give me the thumb of your right hand,' Drona said, his face giving nothing away.

The other princes gasped in horror. What was an archer without his thumb?

But Ekalavya, without the slightest hesitation, drew out his hunting knife and cut off his thumb. Then he held out the bleeding member to Drona who took it wordlessly and left, walking swiftly away. The princes followed in shocked silence, leaving Ekalavya alone in the clearing. Only Arjuna showed no sign of sorrow.

Ekalavya picked up his bow and notched an arrow. Winged shafts flew out with amazing speed and accuracy. The skill was still there but the magic that had marked it was gone for ever. Ekalavya put his bow down and reverently placed some wild flowers on the clay image. In the noble young face there was not a trace of resentment, anger or regret.

Kalidasa's Shakuntala

• *Illustrated by Ajanta Guhathakurta* •

Dushyanta, the mighty Puru King, reigned over an empire that extended from the mountains to the sea. The people lived in great happiness, the seasons marched in their order and the clouds brought rain at the proper time.

One day, the king, who was an avid hunter, went to the forest with a huge retinue of attendants. Chasing an antelope, he charged ahead, leaving his attendants far behind. The fleet little animal took him deep into a densely wooded area and just as the king raised his bow to shoot it down, the frightened antelope bounded into a grove and a voice called out, 'You cannot kill this animal. In this sacred grove nothing is killed.'

The charioteer reined the horses in and the king noticed that the area was filled with an unusual calm and peace. Deer and fawns roamed around quite unafraid of humans. 'This is the hermitage of some great rishi. I am going in, you wait here for me,' he said to his charioteer, taking off his jewels and rich over-cloth. He handed them to the charioteer adding, 'It is not seemly to enter a hermitage dressed so richly.'

As Dushyanta entered the grove his right arm began to throb. 'Am I going to find love here?' wondered the king rubbing his arm. 'Impossible!' He walked on and hearing the joyous laughter of young girls headed towards it. Beyond the trees lay a sylvan garden and in it were three lovely young hermit-maidens dressed in simple bark-fibre clothes, their only ornaments the siris flowers in their ears and a necklace of tender lotus stems. Yet their beauty was radiant, and one, he noticed, was lovelier than the apsaras in heaven. The three girls were watering the young plants in the nursery and the king was enchanted by their artless chatter. He walked out of the shadow of the trees, startling the three maidens who looked at him with wide fearful eyes. One bolder than the others asked him who he was and the king, afraid of scaring them away, said he was the king's inspector. He spoke to her but his eyes never left the lovely girl who stood some distance away.

'Who is this girl who looks like an apsara from Indra's heaven?' he asked her friend.

'She is Shakuntala, Rishi Kanva's daughter,' said the girl with a laughing glance at her friend.

'But the mighty sage has taken a vow not to wed, so how come he has a daughter?' asked the king, truly puzzled.

'She's his adopted daughter,' explained the girl. 'Her father is Vishwamitra, the mighty rishi, and her mother is the heavenly nymph, Menaka. When she was born Menaka left her on the banks of the Malini which flows near our hermitage. Rishi Kanva found her surrounded by birds, and so he called her Shakuntala, after the birds.'

The king chatted with Shakuntala's friends as they watered the plants. Shakuntala said nothing, but looked at him with her heart in her eyes. The plants watered, the girls turned to leave when Shakuntala cried out to her friends, 'Wait for me Anasuya, Priyamvada, this thorny bush has caught my dress!' As she bent to free it, she gave the king a shy look and then ran away.

In the silence that fell the king heard hermits complaining that the king's soldiers were disturbing the peace of the hermitage. 'Oh dear, the men are looking for me. I'd better get them out of here,' he thought as he walked rapidly out of the sacred grove. Sternly he told his men to stop stomping through the grove like bull elephants and ordered them to make camp some distance away. 'The hermits in Rishi Kanva's grove are not to be disturbed.'

The next morning, the commander of the hunt told the king that all was ready but the king had lost his desire for the chase. All he could think of was Shakuntala. He wanted to marry her right away but could not do so without her father's permission. Rishi Kanva was away on a pilgrimage and so all the king could do was wait. Some days later longing for a sight of Shakuntala he went into the hermitage and wandered around looking for her. He found her with her friends on the banks of the Malini in a creeper-covered bower. Shakuntala lay on a slab of stone strewn with flowers, looking pale and ill. Priyamvada and Anasuya sat beside her, fanning her with lotus leaves.

'I must hear what they say,' thought the king hiding himself in the bushes nearby. 'Perhaps my love will speak of me.'

'Is it the heat that has made her ill or her heart?' he heard Anasuya ask Priyamvada. 'Let's ask her,' said Priyamvada. 'Shakuntala, wake up, we must ask you something.'

'What is it?' said Shakuntala weakly.

'I know nothing about love, but in the old legends, the love-lorn one suffers and behaves just like you. Is it the king?' asked Anasuya, for now it was known that the stranger they had met in the garden was none other than the great King Dushyanta himself.

'Oh Anasuya, I don't know,' said Shakuntala, clearly upset, 'but ever since I laid eyes on him I can neither eat nor sleep and my limbs feel heavy and listless. And worse still I have no idea how he feels about me.'

'My dear, you have chosen one worthy of you and he feels the same,' Priyamvada assured her with a loving smile.

'How do you know?' asked Shakuntala tearfully.

'Because I have seen the way his sleepless eyes follow you everywhere,' said Priyamvada. 'Look, why don't you write a letter to him telling him how you feel and I will hide it among the flowers which are taken to him everyday.'

'That's a good idea,' said Anasuya, 'and don't be afraid of doing wrong. It is permitted to marry by the Gandharva rites, Father Kanva will not disapprove. But if you don't, you will pine away.'

'I don't have any writing material,' Shakuntala murmured.

'Here, write on this lotus leaf, engrave the words with your nails.'

'He'll despise me, he'll think I have no modesty,' Shakuntala said, her voice trembling.

'No, he won't,' said her friends robustly, 'he's probably longing for a word from you. Now write.'

Shakuntala sat up and slowly began to write. When it was done she read it out to her friends. 'This is what I have written—"I don't know whether you love me, but night and day, I waste away and can think of nothing but you." Does that sound all right?' she asked anxiously.

The king had heard enough—now that he knew Shakuntala loved him as he loved her, he was determined to marry her right away. He emerged from the bushes and went into the bower. 'O my lovely one, it is more than all right,' he said, his eyes burning, 'love consumes me too, and I want to marry you here and now.'

Shakuntala's friends were delighted to find that the king loved their beloved friend but told him quite clearly he could marry her only if he promised never to bring her any grief, or shame her family in any way.

'I promise I never will,' said the king, 'I love her too much for that.'

Shakuntala married the king and for the next few days met him in secret, keeping the marriage hidden from the hermits in the retreat. Her father, Rishi Kanva, should be the first to know, but there was no sign of the sage and the king could not dally in the forest any longer. There were pressing matters of the state and he had to return to his capital, Hastinapura. 'I will send for you soon,' he told his weeping bride.

'When will that be?' she asked, tears streaming down her moon-white face.

The king took off his ring and slipped it on her finger. 'This ring has my name engraved on it. Count the letters, one for each day, and by the time you reach the last, I will come for you, my beloved.'

The king left and not long after, the mighty Rishi Durvasa came to the hermitage. Shakuntala, sitting on the doorstep, her thoughts far away, did not see the great one standing before her. Neither did she hear his greeting. Durvasa, renowned for his short temper, looked at the day-dreaming girl in fury. 'You do not rise to greet me because your thoughts are on another. The one you think of will forget all about you!' he cursed her and walked away.

Shakuntala's friends who were gathering flowers nearby heard Durvasa cursing her and ran after him and fell at his feet. 'Forgive her, great one, as you would a daughter,' they begged. 'Remove the curse or Rishi Kanva's daughter will surely die.'

The rishi was mollified. 'I can't take back the curse but I can amend it,' he said. 'He will remember her when he sees some token or ornament he has given her.'

'Thank god the king gave her his ring,' said Anasuya to Priyamvada when the rishi vanished, 'he will recognize her as soon as he sees it.'

'Just look at her,' said Priyamvada indulgently, 'sitting there like a painted picture, quite unaware she's been cursed. Let's not tell her about it. She will only worry herself sick.'

Durvasa's curse took effect. Weeks went by and there was no word from the king.

Shakuntala, now pregnant, fretted and pined for her love. One morning she heard the hermits talking excitedly as they went about their duties and knew that her father, Rishi Kanva, was back.

The pious sage greeted his daughter affectionately and wondered at her downcast eyes. Hesitantly, Shakuntala told him about her marriage to King Dushyanta. To her surprise and joy her father was not angry. 'You have wed a worthy man and now that you carry his child, I will send you to him this very day. My chief disciples and Ma Gautami will escort you to the capital.'

A hermitage has many things but not jewels and silks for a bride. Even as her friends wondered how they would dress Shakuntala, hermits came to the cottage with jewels and clothes fit for an empress. 'The trees that she tended with such loving care, produced these for our Shakuntala,' they said handing the trays to the girls.

Now, happily, Anasuya and Priyamvada dressed their beloved friend. When the last fold of silk was twitched into place, they led her to her father. The divine sage blessed his darling child, hiding his sorrow deep in his heart. 'So this is what fathers feel when they send their daughters to their husbands,' he thought grieving silently.

The hermits escorted Shakuntala to the river which marked the boundary of the hermitage. Crying softly, Shakuntala made offerings to the river and then embraced her weeping friends.

'Enough weeping,' said the sage, 'send her with cheer and good wishes.'

'Show the ring to the king as soon as you see him,' her friends told her with a serious look. 'Don't forget to do that.'

The words made Shakuntala afraid but her friends would say no more. When the tearful farewells were over, Shakuntala left the forest with her escort.

In Hastinapura, the king, who had lost all memory of Shakuntala, passed his days in a state of abject joylessness though he did not know its cause. 'What does my heart want?' he wondered.

One day the chamberlain came to him with the news that hermits from Rishi Kanva had arrived at the palace. 'Take them to the court with all due honour. I will be there to receive them.'

When the hermits entered the magnificent court, the king's eyes fell on the veiled Shakuntala and he wondered who this unearthly beauty was. 'Welcome,' he said rising, 'Is all well with Rishi Kanva?'

Shakuntala saw her husband look at her with the eyes of a stranger and a nameless fear gripped her.

'We have brought your wife, Rishi Kanva's daughter, Shakuntala, to you, as is proper,' said the chief disciple. 'She will soon be the mother of your child.'

'My wife? My child?' asked the astonished king. 'But I haven't married the sage's daughter. I don't even know her!'

'How can you forget?' the hermit asked sternly. 'Is this the way of honourable kings—to entice innocent maids in forest retreats? Look at her, she is the girl you married.'

Gautami unveiled Shakuntala's face. 'O God! If I had married this flawless beauty, I would never have left her,' thought the king staring at Shakuntala. 'Holy ones, I have not married this lady,' he said. 'I have never seen her before. Is this some ruse?'

Shakuntala looked at him, stunned by the denial. Then the king's veiled insults roused her anger.

'You deny you married me but I will show you something which will bring the truth out,' she said raising her hand and her eyes widened in horror. 'Oh Ma, I have lost the ring he gave me, it must have fallen into the river when I offered it worship!' she cried out, tears welling in her eyes.

The king's lip curled in a cruel smile. 'You are beautiful and very clever. First you claim I gave you a ring, now you say you have lost it! How very convenient.'

The pious hermits were enraged by the king's insults. 'Let's go. Shakuntala must stay, she married him, and the king must do what he pleases! Come Ma Gautami,' said the eldest as they strode out of the court.

Shakuntala followed them out weeping piteously. 'You can't leave me here,' she cried, 'he's rejected me! Where will I go?'

But the hermits walked on turning a deaf ear to her cries. The king's chamberlain who had followed Shakuntala saw a beam of light shoot down from the sky. A beautiful woman stepped out and wrapping her arms around Shakuntala flew off with her into the heavens. He told the king what he had seen but the king showed no interest.

The days and years passed. King Dushyanta reigned as he should, but life held no pleasure for him. One day a policeman came to court with a poor fisherman in tow.

'This man has your ring, sire,' said the policeman. 'He must have stolen it though he denies it, saying he found it in the stomach of a carp.'

He gave the king the ring and the moment Dushyanta saw it his memory came flooding back. He remembered everything—the first time he saw Shakuntala, his marriage to her and the terrible insults he had heaped on her. Guilt and remorse and a terrible ache filled him. Where could he look for her? A divine being had flown off with her but where, no one knew. Burdened by guilt and sorrow, the king banned all festivities in the kingdom.

Walking alone in the garden one day, a shining chariot came flying down from the sky. 'Matali?' exclaimed the king when he saw Indra's charioteer. 'What brings you here?'

'The asuras have attacked the heavens and Indra needs some help,' said Matali. 'Come, we must leave immediately.'

The king had no heart for festivity or battle but he could not refuse the god of the thunderbolt. He went with Matali and fought the asuras. When the battle was over, Matali said he would take him back. As they flew down to earth the chariot passed over a wondrous mountain. 'What is that peak?' asked king.

'That is Hema-Kuta, the home of Kashyapa, father of the gods and the asuras and all mankind,' said Matali flying down. 'Indra said I am to take you there before I take you back to Hastinapura.'

They alighted in a beautiful grove of trees and Matali asked the king to wait. 'I will go and see if Brahma's son is within.'

As the king sat down in the shade of a tree, his right arm began to throb. 'Why does my arm throb? Only to remind me of my lost love, I suppose.' He sat there brooding over his harsh words to Shakuntala when he heard a scolding female voice.

'Stop that naughty behaviour! You're back to your wild ways, you naughty child!'

A little boy came running into the grove, dragging a half-grown lion cub by the tail. Behind him ran two harassed lady-ascetics, clucking and scolding. The king looked at the child with a smile. 'Brave little fellow,' he thought as he watched the little boy trying to open the cub's jaws.

'Open your mouth,' the boy shouted in a childish treble. 'I want to count your teeth!'

'Stop tormenting that poor cub,' scolded one lady. 'His mother will come and attack you if you don't let him go.'

'And of course I am scared,' said the little boy scowling at her. 'I want to count his teeth! Open your mouth,' the child repeated.

'This is no hermit's son,' thought the king. 'And why does my heart reach out to him?'

'Let the cub go and I will give you another toy,' coaxed the other lady.

'Give it to me first,' said the little boy holding out his hands and the king saw the marks of royalty on them.

'Lucky is the king who has a son such as this,' thought Dushyanta with a sad smile.

One lady left the grove while the other tried to free the cub but to no avail. Then she caught sight of the king and said, 'Kind sir, please get the cub away from this boy. He'll maul it to death.'

Dushyanta rose and very easily took the cub away from the boy and hoisted him up into his arms as the little animal scampered away.

'Who is this boy? He does not seem to be the child of a hermitage,' the king asked.

'Oh no, he's not, though he was born here,' said the lady looking at the king in surprise. 'He has never let a stranger hold him before.'

'Who is the child's father?' asked the king, he simply had to know.

'I don't want to mention that awful man's name,' said the lady with marked displeasure. Then she looked at the child and clicked her tongue in annoyance. 'He's lost his amulet. Careless child!'

The king stooped down. 'He dropped it when he was playing with the cub,' he said picking it up even as the lady cried, 'Don't touch it!'

Then she looked at the king in amazement. 'It turns into a serpent if anyone but his parents touch it,' she said slowly. 'Oh I must go and tell Shakuntala you're here!'

'I want to go to mama,' said the child struggling in the stunned king's arms. 'Shakuntala! She's here! I have found my love,' ran his thoughts even as he said, 'Come, we will go to her together. I am your father, my son.'

'You are not my father, Dushyanta is,' said the little boy pouting angrily at him.

'Yes, you are Dushyanta's son,' said the king with a shaky laugh and put him down.

'Mama!' the boy cried and darted off.

The king turned and saw Shakuntala enter the grove with the lady-hermits. Pale and slender, she was dressed in simple clothes, with no ornaments on her neck or flowers in her hair.

Shakuntala saw the king and stood still, holding her son in trembling hands. 'Who is this man who calls me son?' asked the child tugging at her garment.

'Fate has taken pity on me,' thought Shakuntala as tears streamed down her face.

The king went to her and held her close. 'Oh my love, my heart, can you forgive me?' he murmured brokenly. 'I still don't understand how I could have forgotten you.'

Matali then took the king to Kashyapa who told him about Durvasa's curse. 'It was not your fault you forgot your wife,' said the First Father with a smile. 'Return to Hastinapura with your family. We call your son the "tamer of wild beasts", but he shall be called Bharata,' stated Brahma's son.

Matali took the royal family back to earth and the king and his beautiful queen lived happily for many a long year. Bharata succeeded his father and became the greatest king the world had ever seen. And the land he ruled over forever bears his name—Bharata.

The magic pot

• *Illustrated by Neeta Gangopadhya* •

In the ancient city of Pataliputra, there once lived a poor woodcutter called Subha. Every morning the wretched man went into the forest, chopped as much wood as he could carry and sold it in the market. But the few coins he earned were hardly enough to feed his family and they often went to sleep worn out with hunger.

One day, when he was chopping a fallen log, he heard voices in the nearby glade. Putting down his axe he went to the edge and saw four radiantly handsome men with clothes that shimmered as if woven from moonbeams. 'Oh my god! They're Yakshas,' he whispered to himself.

'Yes we are,' said one turning towards the bush Subha was hiding behind. 'Don't be afraid, show yourself.'

The divine beings looked at the scrawny man in his tattered clothes with kindness and pity. 'Who are you?' they asked.

'I'm Subha, the woodcutter,' he said trembling with fear. 'O divine ones, don't harm a poor man like me.'

'We have no such intention,' said the Yakshas. 'Since you are so poor, work for us and we will make you rich.'

'You will?' Subha exclaimed. 'Then I'll surely work with you, divine ones,' he said, bowing.

'Hold my hand and close your eyes,' said one of them.

When Subha opened his eyes a moment later, he was in a fabulous palace with golden pillars and lapis floors.

'You will wait on us,' the Yakshas said, handing him an ordinary clay pot. 'Whatever we want, food or drink or anything else, you will get from this pot.'

'But it is empty, masters,' Subha said peering in.

'It will provide when needed,' the Yakshas said, amused. 'Put your hand in and wish for something, anything.'

'What I would like is some kheer,' Subha breathed and the pot brimmed over with the delicious sweet.

'It's as you said, masters!' he exclaimed wonderstruck.

Subha served the Yakshas for a long time, doing whatever they asked of him, and all that they desired he got from the pot, whether food or jewels, wine or flowers.

But as the days slipped by Subha began to miss his wife and children and the Yakshas noticed he no longer smiled when he served them.

'Why are you sad?' they asked.

'I miss my family,' Subha said, shuffling his feet.

'Then it is time you went home,' the Yakshas said kindly. 'Before you leave, we will grant you a boon. Ask for whatever you want.'

'I want the clay pot,' Subha said without hesitation.

At that the Yakshas grew grave. 'Ask for something else, fine gems and gold, but forget about the pot,' they advised. 'The pot will not do you much good in the long run.'

'I want the pot,' Subha insisted stubbornly.

'Change your mind Subha. If you break the pot you will lose everything. We will give you all the gold and gems you can carry.'

'I want the pot,' Subha repeated. 'It will give me all I want anyway.'

'And more, much more,' said the Yakshas with a strange look which Subha did not notice.

A happy Subha returned home and told his family about his adventure with the Yakshas and the magic pot. 'This nondescript clay pot will give us everything. We will be rich and I won't have to work ever again.'

Subha very soon became enormously wealthy and the neighbours wondered where the wealth had come from. 'Let's ask him,' said one. 'Subha is a nice chap, he'll tell us.'

But when Subha saw his poor neighbours in his fine courtyard, he looked at them as if they were unwelcome strangers. The pot had given him more than wealth, he was now proud and rude and vain. 'Why are you here?' he asked arrogantly.

'We want to know how you've become so rich so suddenly?' they said.

'It's none of your business,' Subha said rudely, 'but since you ask, I get my wealth from a magic pot. Now that you know, you can go.'

Things changed. Though Subha was rich, no friends came to visit him but he didn't care, he had his pot. One day he asked the pot for some fine red wine and drank his fill. Then he rose tipsily and began dancing around the room with the pot on his head. As he lurched around, he tripped over a footstool and fell. The pot broke and its shards rose into the air and flew out of the window and as they left all the things that had come from it vanished as if they had never been. Subha found himself back in his poor little hut with his hungry children wailing for food. Now he knew what the Yakshas had meant when they had said, 'You will get much more.'

Poor once more, he went to the forest everyday to chop wood, hoping to see the Yakshas again. But you don't get lucky every day and he remained a poor woodcutter all his life.

Naranth Prandhan and Bhadrakali

• *Illustrated by Tapas Guha* •

Naranth was the son of Vararuchi, the great brahmin scholar from the court of King Vikramaditya. When Vararuchi left the king's court he went to Kerala, married and had twelve sons. One of them was Naranth Prandhan.

Prandhan did the strangest of things. Every day he rolled a boulder up a hill only to throw it down. And when it fell, he would laugh and jump around like a mad man. Sometimes he spent days just watching ants. All the villagers thought he was crazy and called him Prandhan, which means a mad man. But mad he was not.

Prandhan had other peculiar habits. He never worked, and always got his food by begging. When there was enough, he stopped, though he could have got plenty more. After collecting his rice, vegetables and lentils, Prandhan went around looking for a fire. Where he found one, there he cooked, where he cooked, there he ate and where he ate, there he slept. This routine was strictly followed.

One evening after getting some rice and vegetables Prandhan went looking for a fire. There was none in the village square, nothing in the maidan. Prandhan walked out of the village and in the crematorium he saw a blazing funeral pyre.

'There's my fire,' he thought walking in. He made a makeshift stove with some stones, pulled out some glowing embers and burning faggots, put them in the stove and set his pot of rice to boil. That done, Prandhan sat down and with a great sigh settled his right leg on the warm stones. That leg was diseased with elephantiasis which makes the limbs balloon up and look much like an elephant's. The warmth was very soothing and Prandhan leaned back and closed his eyes. The pyre went on with its crackling, the rice and vegetables went on with their bubbling and Prandhan with his resting. All was quiet and peaceful. Suddenly the serenity was shattered by blood-curdling screams, beating drums and clashing cymbals.

Prandhan opened one eye and what he saw made the other fly open. Bhadrakali with her hoard of demonesses came in. They were here to dance, sing and feast at the funeral pyre. That was their business and they went about it with great enthusiasm.

Prandhan looked, shrugged his shoulders and stirred the rice and vegetables. 'A little more and it's done,' he murmured to himself.

Bhadrakali and her demonesses began their wild dance around the pyre, their hair snaking, red eyes gleaming and their fangs shining white in the firelight.

Kali abruptly stopped her whirling, slamming into the demonesses behind her. 'There's a human sitting there,' she said to her minions. 'How dare he!' Then raising her voice, the fierce goddess called out, 'Mortal! What are you doing here?'

'Can't you see, lady?' Prandhan asked with scant respect. 'I'm cooking my food.'

'Leave this place at once,' the terrible goddess commanded, 'or else…'

Any sensible man would have bolted, but Prandhan just sat there and stared at her, a mulish expression on his face. 'Sorry lady, I was here first and I'm not leaving. As you can see, I'm cooking my food and then I'm going to eat it here.'

Bhadrakali was flabbergasted first, then furious. 'I'm going to scare the living daylights out of you and you'll run like a hunted hare!'

Prandhan's mulish expression grew even more mulish. 'Terrorize all you want, lady, but I'm not going anywhere,' he said flatly.

Bhadrakali was stunned—this stupid man didn't have the sense to be scared of her! 'Humans quiver like peepal leaves in the wind when they see me,' she thundered.

'I don't know about other people, but I'm not about to be scared into leaving,' said Prandhan coolly.

Bhadrakali and her creatures put on a show that would have blanched a ghost. They thrust their horrid, nasty faces into his, screaming and screeching, raking the air with their claws. A wind sprang up howling and raging and tiny whirlwinds sprang up and danced around Prandhan. But he didn't budge, he sat scowling at them. Then fed up with all the noise, he banged his ladle on a stone.

'Hurry up and finish this business of frightening me,' he shouted impatiently. 'I'm hungry and I want to eat.'

The goddess went rigid with shock. Had she been human she would have stood gawking with her mouth hanging open. But goddesses don't gawk. 'This is no mere mortal. This one's special. I must make a deal with him,' she thought. 'Why don't you go now,' she cajoled Prandhan. 'We must sing and dance around those who have gone to Yama. You can return some other time.'

'Madam, as I said earlier—I—am—not—going—to—leave,' he said clearly as if explaining to a half-wit. 'You go ahead with your dancing and singing, I'm not stopping you but I stay here.'

'No mortal eyes may see our ritual dance,' the goddess said, almost wheedling. 'You must go, please.'

'If that's the case, you leave and return tomorrow,' Prandhan retorted. 'I won't be here and you can dance all you like.'

'We must dance the day the pyre is lit,' the goddess explained. 'This law is unchangeable and our guiding principle.'

'Well, I too have some principles which can't be changed,' came the smart rejoinder. 'I beg for my food every evening. When I've got enough I look for a fire. Where I find the fire I cook, where I cook I eat, where I eat I sleep. That

stands firm, like Mount Sumeru.'

Kali knew she had met her match. 'Very well, I have to visit another funeral pyre anyway and so I'll leave,' she said with whatever remained of her dignity. 'But I must grant you a boon before I go. Ask.'

'There's nothing I want except to eat my dinner in peace,' Prandhan said impatiently.

'But you must ask for something,' said the flustered goddess. 'I must stay till you do.'

'In that case, I'd better ask you for something,' he said wearily. 'Tell me, do you know when I'm going to die?'

'Of course, you will die after thirty-six years, six months, twelve days and three seconds,' Kali answered promptly.

'Right then—since you must give me something, give me one more day to live.'

'That's impossible!' exclaimed the goddess. 'Even I can't change the time when Death will come to you. I can't give you a second more.'

'In that case give me one day less to live,' Prandhan said, looking fed up.

'I can't do that either,' Kali admitted.

'Then why are you bothering me with your stupid boon when you can't give anything I ask for,' Prandhan snapped at her. 'I didn't want anything in the first place.'

'Please, ask for something I can grant,' Kali practically pleaded.

'I've got to get rid of her,' thought Prandhan. 'As you can see, my right leg is diseased, just shift the disease to my left leg. That will make a change,' he said.

Visibly relieved, Kali granted his request. Prandhan's left leg swelled up, his right leg shrank to its normal size and Kali vanished. Prandhan equally relieved, sat back. He stirred the pot, dinner was ready. 'Nothing like eating a meal in peace,' he thought and with a contented sigh placed his left leg on the warm stones and began to eat.

The rabbit who fooled the elephant

• *Illustrated by Jaishree Misra* •

Deep in a forest lived an elephant-king surrounded by his mighty herd. He was a good ruler who protected his cows and calves and the herd was happy.

Then came a terrible time. Drought hit the land and the pools and ponds, the lakes and swamps all dried up.

The elephants, weak with thirst, went to their king and said, 'Lord, the children are dying without water. Some are already dead, so please do something.'

The elephant-king sent for his attendants. 'Go out in all four directions and look for water,' he commanded.

The elephants who went towards the east at last came to a hermitage. Nearby, hidden among the trees, was a spring-fed lake which had escaped the long years of drought. Cool, crystal-clear water lapped the shores, lotuses of every hue covered its surface and ducks and waterfowl glided on shimmering waters. The elephants however didn't stop to drink. Checking the lake's position, they hurried back to tell their king about the pool.

'We will leave immediately,' the elephant-king said as soon as his scouts brought their reports.

The herd travelled for five days and nights and on the sixth day reached the hidden lake. Cows, calves and bull-elephants all plunged into the clear waters and when they had bathed and drunk their fill, stepped onto the sandy shore. Now in the soft sand were countless rabbit burrows and the elephants' enormous feet crushed hundreds of rabbits as they walked away.

When the herd left, the surviving rabbits, wounded, angry and covered with blood met in a council. 'This is the end of us. All the lakes except this one are dry, so that herd will come here every day. Most of us lie dead; one more visit and we'll all be dead. The wise say that an elephant's touch, a cobra's breath and a king's smile all bring death. To save ourselves we'll have to do something drastic,' said the elders.

One timid rabbit was the first to speak. 'I think we should leave our homes and find another place far away from the elephants. What else can we do? We're just little rabbits, we can't fight a herd of elephants.'

But the others protested. 'This is the land of our forefathers. We can't leave simply because a herd of elephants has found our hidden lake. No, instead of leaving, we

must find a way to drive the herd away.'

For a while there was silence. Then an old rabbit, known for his wisdom, said, 'I have a plan but it needs a brave person who can act and has a way with words.'

'What is it?' asked the others eagerly. Any plan was better than none.

The old rabbit looked up at the darkening sky. Soon the full moon would rise. 'We need someone to make the elephant-king believe that our king lives in the moon, and that this lake belongs to the Moon God. He must convince him that the Moon God has forbidden elephants to come to the lake, and that, if they don't go away, our king will be forced to take action against the elephants. This hopefully, will scare the elephants and the elephant-king won't dare bring his herd here again.'

Now arose the problem of whom to send. After much arguing the council decided on a rabbit named Lamba Karan. 'He's a clever fellow and a smooth talker. More important, he is brave. He'll take the false message to the king of the elephants.'

Lamba Karan, which literally means long ears, was a scrawny chap, small even for a rabbit. He hardly looked the hero, but then looks have nothing to do with being a braveheart. It's courage that counts.

The full moon rose, fat and golden, and Lamba Karan set off. He walked briskly along the forest path until he came to a steep slope and climbing up he saw the herd under the trees.

'O king of elephants!' he called out. 'Aren't you afraid of the Moon God's wrath? You have been mucking up the water, playing and splashing about in his lake. You'd better go away before he gets angry.'

The elephant-king rose to his full height, towering over the puny rabbit. His tusks gleamed, white and dangerous.

'Who are you?' he bellowed in anger, making the trees tremble.

'I am Vijaydutt, the Rabbit in the Moon. I've come here with a message from the Moon God. And remember, I'm only a messenger, the words are the Moon God's. The god does not want you to play in his lake any more.'

The elephant-king's little eyes were like red points in his dark head.

'No point losing your temper with me,' the little rabbit said quickly, when he saw the fiery gleam in the elephant-king's eyes, 'I'm only an envoy.'

'All right, what is the Moon God's message?' the elephant-king rumbled.

The rabbit bowed and said, '"You have killed my rabbits in great numbers. If you want to live never come to the lake again, and leave the forest immediately." This is the Moon God's command.'

The elephant-king was not easily fooled. 'Where is the Moon God now?' he asked.

'At the moment he's in the lake,' replied the rabbit.

'If that's true, take me to him,' said the elephant, 'and if he's really in the lake, I'll go away.'

The rabbit and the elephant-king walked down the moonlit path to the shores of the lake. In the black waters, a bright disc shimmered, silvering the surface with bits of moonlight.

The rabbit raised a paw, stopping the elephant-king in his tracks. Pointing to the moon's reflection, he whispered, 'There's the Moon God. Don't disturb him, he's meditating. Pay your respects quietly and go. If he's disturbed you and your herd will perish.'

The elephant looked at the silvery disc in awe and fear. The Moon God was really in the lake! He went down on his knees and bowed low. Then he rose and quietly walked away with his herd. As soon as he'd gone, the rabbit danced in glee. 'He swallowed the whole story! He's gone!'

From that day the rabbits lived happily on the shores of the hidden lake and are probably still there.

Bhima and Vakasura

• *Illustrated by Prithvishwar Gayen* •

The Kuru princes graduated and left their guru's home to begin their lives in the world beyond. But back in the palace Duryodhana's suppressed hatred of his cousins surfaced and it was no longer a childish hate but one that had grown and matured. All pretence was shed and plans were made to kill Pandu's queen and his five sons.

'They shan't live to lay claims to the throne,' Duryodhana swore.

But to set the plan in motion, he needed his father's help and though the blind king knew that his sons were up to no good he agreed to do as Duryodhana asked. 'Send them to Varanavata, father,' Duryodhana told the king. 'Let them all have a holiday. It's a beautiful city and with the festival season drawing near, they are sure to enjoy themselves. We will then…'

'I don't want to hear any details,' the king interrupted. 'But take care, the people of Hastinapura love Pandu's sons dearly.'

'Once they are out of the way, I'll buy the goodwill of the people if I must,' was Duryodhana's sneaky solution.

The blind king put up a feeble argument which Duryodhana dismissed carelessly and the old king buckled. He sent for the Pandavas and Kunti and told them they ought to go to Varanavata for a holiday. The Pandavas knew that there was something afoot but they went anyhow. They had little choice but to obey the king. In the meanwhile, Duryodhana had his men construct a fabulous mansion made of lac, straw-bricks and wood—everything that could burn. When the Pandavas and Kunti reached Varanavata they were taken to the mansion but Yudhishthira noticed that no stone or clay bricks had been used. With the help of a miner sent by their uncle Vidura they secretly made an underground tunnel which led into a forest. One night when all were asleep, Duryodhana's men set fire to the mansion and the flames licked the sky, lighting up the city. News that Pandu's sons and his queen had died in a fire quickly reached Hastinapura and the Kauravas shed crocodile tears and pretended to mourn their dead cousins.

But the Pandavas and Kunti escaped through the tunnel and a boatman ferried them across the river to the deep forest on the other bank. Once there, the princes and the queen took off their royal garments and put on clothes made of bark fibre such as wandering mendicants wore. They let their hair grow and become matted and the harsh jungle life toughened their hands and feet. Now they no longer looked like royal princes but ascetic brahmins who begged for a living. The Pandavas realized it was pointless returning to Hastinapura until they were in a stronger position—Duryodhana would only try to kill them again and his father would not stop him or give them their rightful position.

'What do we do now?' Arjuna asked, tying his matted hair into a topknot. 'We can't skulk in this forest forever.'

'I don't know,' Yudhishthira said wearily.

Just then Ved Vyasa, the sage, entered their hermitage and the Pandavas greeted him joyously, happy to see a dear familiar face in the wilderness.

'Keep your chins up,' Vyasa said to his grandsons, for he was Bhishma's stepbrother. 'I know about Duryodhana's attempt to murder you. Right now, there is nothing you can do except lie low. Don't let anyone know you are alive. Go to the nearby town of Ekachakra and live there for a while. Keep your disguises—if Duryodhana finds out you are alive he'll send his hit squad after you. And don't worry, the time will come when you will take your rightful place in Hastinapura.'

Kunti and the Pandavas went to Ekachakra and found shelter with a poor brahmin family. Their host had no suspicion about their true identities. Every morning the Pandavas went out to beg for alms and returned at dusk. They gave all the food they received to Kunti who divided it among them. One half was given to Bhima and the rest she divided between the other four, keeping a small portion for herself. They lived a quiet life and kept to themselves, doing nothing that would draw attention to them.

Late one morning Kunti heard people weeping in the brahmin's room. Only Bhima was in because he had not yet finished his meal. 'I'm going to find out what has happened,' she said to him. 'We owe this brahmin a great deal. Perhaps the time has come to pay our debt. Stay here till I return.'

Kunti went to the brahmin's door and finding it open went in. There she saw the whole family weeping bitterly. Only the youngest son was prancing around saying, 'Send me father, I'll kill that nasty rakshasa who eats people!' His mother grabbed him and held him close.

'What is the matter?' Kunti asked. 'Why are you all weeping?'

The brahmin looked up when he heard her voice. 'We have reason to weep,' the man said brokenly. 'Tomorrow one of us is going to die.'

'Why?' asked Kunti astonished.

'In the forest beyond the city lives a mighty asura called Vaka, also known as Vakasura. He protects our town from the other asuras and as payment the town's people send him a cartload of rice and curry, two buffaloes and one human being. That's his daily meal and families take turns to supply him. Tomorrow it's my turn,' he said starkly.

'You cannot die,' wept his wife. 'I don't want to live as your widow. Let me go.'

'I'll go mother,' said the young daughter. 'My brother is young still and needs you. I can be spared.'

'No, my dear, no,' said the brahmin. 'My children shall not die before me.'

'Nobody here is going to die,' Kunti said calmly. Taking the brahmin aside she said, 'You have one son, I have five. One of them will drive the cart tomorrow.'

'Oh no,' the brahmin cried, horrified. 'I can't sacrifice your son to save my life. He's my guest, guests are sacred!'

'Yes they are,' Kunti agreed, 'but I assure you, no harm will come to my son.' Her tone grew softer. 'The gods have given him enormous strength, he will be in no danger.'

'No, lady, no,' the brahmin protested, 'Vaka will kill him.'

'What I am going to tell you now is secret, you must not tell a soul,' Kunti went on, ignoring the protest. 'My son is so strong that asuras fear him, but if anyone comes to know he has used his superhuman strength, his guru will be very annoyed. And he may lose his strength if that happens.'

Kunti lied without batting an eyelid. She had to, to protect her sons. If Duryodhana's spies got wind of a poor mendicant brahmin who could kill demons, they would surely smell a rat and the assassins would be after them again. But she also had to help the kind brahmin who had given her family shelter. And so she lied. 'No one must know who has taken the cart, not even the town elders. When the deed is done, tell them that a stranger helped you. Have the cart ready in the morning. And don't worry, all will be well.'

Kunti went back and told Bhima about Vakasura. 'I want you to deal with this,' she said. 'We owe the brahmin and must save his life. You will take the cart to the forest.'

'With pleasure, mother,' Bhima said, flexing his powerful muscles which were usually hidden under a cotton shawl. 'This tranquil life doesn't really agree with me, I need the exercise,' he added with a wide grin.

'Do it quietly,' Kunti said sternly. 'No one must see you behaving like a kshatriya warrior.'

Early next morning, Bhima was up before the birds and Kunti led him to the cart. 'I'll be back soon,' he said to her as he drove off.

The buffaloes were fresh and they bowled along at a spanking pace, that is a buffalo's spanking pace. He entered the forest just as the sun was beginning to turn the grey leaves into green and the grey sky into blue. When he reached Vaka's cave he drew in the reins and parked the cart near the mouth. 'Vaka! Vaka!' he bellowed. 'Breakfast is here, come and get it!'

Bhima's thundering cry startled the birds out of the trees and the deer in the glade. When the monster didn't emerge he shouted again, 'Vaka! Come out you slobbering lump of ugliness!'

There was still no answer. Bhima looked at the delicious rice and curry and wiped his hands on his shawl. 'Must not let this good food spoil,' he thought virtuously. 'Now *that* would be a crime.'

Bhima began to eat, stopping every now and then to yell out 'Vaka'. When he was almost done he heard the heavy pounding of gigantic feet. Vaka burst out of the cave, his red eyes rolling. The sight of Bhima casually eating his food was more than he could take.

'That is my food you are eating!' he roared, 'and you have finished it all!'

'You still have the buffaloes and me,' Bhima laughed as he dusted his hands.

'I'll eat you first,' snarled the furious asura.

'You can try,' Bhima said sweetly, jumping down from the cart.

Vaka tore out a tree and hurled it at Bhima as if it was a lightweight javelin. Bhima nimbly stepped aside and tearing out a tree hurled it at Vaka.

Vaka's eyes popped out in surprise when he saw a tree hurtling towards him. 'This can't be happening, that's my meal attacking me!'

Tree after tree was uprooted and hurled and animals fled as the two battled it out. Finally Bhima got close enough to Vaka and seized him in a vice-like grip. Whirling him in the air he flung him down, pinning the asura between his knees. Then he raised Vaka's torso and snapped his spine. Vaka died screaming in agony. Bhima rose, heaved the body into the cart and drove back to town. It was still early when he entered the city gate, not even the milkmen were up. Making sure there was no one around, Bhima left the body there and made his way back home.

The news of Vaka's death spread through Ekachakra like a forest fire. People poured out of their houses to look at the corpse, not quite believing the reign of terror was over. Then the elders went to the brahmin's house. 'Who went in your place? Who killed Vaka?' they asked.

'A stranger found me weeping and offered to save my life,' the brahmin lied coolly. 'And I didn't even stop to ask his name.'

Kunti and the Pandavas, who were standing in the yard, smiled. The good man had lied like a trooper, even though it had gone against his grain.

The jasmine princess

• Illustrated by Bindia Thapar •

There once lived a king who had only one son and he loved him dearly. The prince grew into a handsome young man and the king thought it was time he wed. But before any plans could be made the snakes in the kingdom began to create havoc. The king was now worried about his subjects who were dying by the score. There were snakes everywhere and people were afraid to sleep at night or go out during the day. The prince decided to take matters into his own hands and with a band of brave and trusty soldiers went all over the land hunting and killing snakes. One day when they were in a forest the tired prince went to sleep under a tree. As he slept a great big snake with seven hoods came slithering down the trunk. The prince's men were about to kill it when he woke up and stopped them. The great snake looked at him with pain-filled eyes.

'What do you want from me, king of snakes?' the prince asked.

'I have a terrible headache. I've been suffering for seven long years and the pain is so bad I can't keep my subjects in order,' groaned the mighty serpent.

'So this is why the snakes are creating so much trouble,' said the prince. 'Can't you do something about this headache?'

'Only one thing can cure it—the scent of the jasmine that falls out of the mouth of the Jasmine Princess.'

'Who is this Jasmine Princess?' asked the prince, intrigued.

'Far away in the south there lies a great kingdom. The king has only one daughter—a beautiful delicate princess who weighs only as much as seven handfuls of jasmine flowers. When she laughs, three divine jasmines drop from her mouth, but she hasn't laughed for many years. The scent of those divine jasmines will cure my headache and then your kingdom will not be troubled by snakes anymore.'

'I'll find her and bring the flowers,' the prince swore.

The prince and his band of trusty men headed south. On the way the prince stopped at a pond to drink some water when he saw a big ant struggling in the shallows. Gently he picked the tiny creature up and set it down on the grass.

'I am the king of ants and I thank you for saving my life,' the ant said. 'If you ever need my help, think of me and I'll be there.'

A few days later, riding through a forest, the prince heard a horrible cry. He searched the area and came across a gigantic demon with a tamarind tree growing out of its mouth. The awful cries were coming from him. The prince saw that the tree had rooted the demon to the ground. He cut the tree down and helped the demon get the roots out of its mouth.

'Thank you,' said the demon bowing. 'If you ever need my help, think of me and I'll be there,' he said and flew off.

At last the prince reached the kingdom of the Jasmine Princess. He went to the palace and was taken to the king. 'I am the prince of a faraway land and I've come here because I want to marry your daughter,' said the prince.

'There are three tasks you must perform and if you do, you can marry her,' said the king.

The prince, who had had a long time to think about the

fragile little princess, now wanted her for herself and not just for the divine jasmines that fell from her mouth. And so he said, 'I'll do whatever you ask.'

'Tonight, my men will bring a hundred sacks of rice and black gram, all mixed up. You must separate them by dawn.'

That evening the servants took him to a barn where there were a hundred sacks of rice and gram. The prince looked at the black and white grain and wondered how on earth he was going to separate them when he thought of the ant king. In a moment the ant king stood near his foot. 'Why have you called me?' he asked the prince.

'I must separate the rice from the gram by dawn,' said the prince.

'That's easily done,' said the ant king.

The prince emptied the sacks on the floor and soon tens of thousands of ants poured into the barn and got down to work. By dawn there were two piles in the barn, one white and one black.

The king was very pleased. None of his daughter's suitors had got this far. 'Today I will send one hundred types of pullao and a hundred glasses of buttermilk to your chamber. You must eat all the pullao and drink all the buttermilk by dawn.'

In the evening the king's cooks brought a hundred big bowls of pullao and a hundred glasses of buttermilk to the prince's chamber.

'Enjoy your dinner,' they said with a snigger and left.

As soon as he was alone the prince thought of the demon who appeared at once. 'Why did you call?' asked the demon.

'To give you dinner,' the prince said with a grin.

'That is most kind,' said the demon greedily eyeing the food.

He demolished the pullao in five bites and drank up the buttermilk in one gulp. 'Thank you,' he burped, 'and excuse me, that was excellent pullao.'

In the morning the king came to the prince's chamber and found all the dishes lying empty. 'Excellent!' he said. 'And now for the third task. Tonight we celebrate the festival of Shiva. Beyond the city lies a hill and on that hill there is a golden bell. When the bell is rung, it can be heard seven kingdoms away. You must ring that bell at midnight.'

The prince rode out of the city and up the hill. Anyone can ring a bell, he thought. When he reached the top he saw the bell, and what a bell it was! It towered into the sky almost touching the clouds. The prince knew he would not be able to even move it and once again he thought of the demon. The demon appeared at once. 'What do you want me to do now?' he asked.

'I want you to ring this bell at midnight,' said the prince.

'Is that all?' said the demon easily picking up the bell.

When the full moon rode high in the night sky, the demon rang the bell and the king, seven kingdoms away, sat up in his bed.

The prince returned to the palace and the next morning, when all were in court, the Jasmine Princess came in. When the prince saw her his heart beat furiously. 'If the snake king didn't have his headache, the snakes would have never troubled my kingdom, and I would have never seen her,' he thought gazing at the fragile beauty.

'As promised, you will marry my beloved child today,' said the king. 'But if you can make her laugh before she leaves me, I will be in your debt.'

'That I will do,' said the prince and he was married to the solemn little princess who weighed no more than seven handfuls of jasmine blossoms. The next morning, the prince sent one of his men into the city. 'Find a man with a monkey that can do tricks,' he ordered. 'Have them at the palace gates.'

The king gave the prince and his bride a splendid send-off and walked with them to the gates of his palace. 'You must bring my daughter to visit me as often as you can,' he said to the prince.

As they reached the gates, the princess caught sight of the monkey and looked at it curiously. Then the monkey began to somersault and dance in such a comical fashion that the princess began to smile. The smile grew broader and broader and soon she was laughing. As her pearly teeth flashed, three jasmines fell from her mouth and the prince hastily picked them up.

'I have done the last thing you asked of me,' the prince said to the king. 'Now I must return to my father's kingdom.'

The prince and his party rode as fast at they could and when they reached his kingdom they went to the forest. The serpent-king was still in the tree, groaning with pain. The prince held the divine jasmines to his nose and the seven-year headache disappeared. 'For this I will give you a magic jewel,' said the grateful king of snakes. 'Whenever you need me, look into it and think of me,' he said handing the prince a beautiful blue gem, 'I will be with you in a trice.'

The prince bowed to him and finally took his bride home. The snakes stopped troubling the kingdom and the prince and the Jasmine Princess lived happily for many a long year.

How Ganesha got his elephant head

• *Illustrated by Ajanta Guhathakurta* •

Parvati, daughter of Himavat, wife of Shiva, had one pet dislike—being interrupted when she was bathing. And Shiva often came barging in when he had no business to. One day when Shiva was away, Parvati rubbed her body with jasmine oil and sandalpaste. 'This time he shan't burst in when I have a bath,' she thought as she scraped off the scented paste from her limbs. She kneaded the perfumed lump and made a little paste boy, then holding it close to her lips, she breathed life into it. In the time it takes to blink, the child became a handsome young boy and he looked at his mother with wondering eyes. Parvati embraced her son and said, 'I'm going for a bath now. Don't let anyone enter this chamber.'

'Yes, mother,' the boy said, posting himself at the door, and stood with his sturdy young legs firmly apart.

Parvati went in for a long, leisurely bath.

Shiva returning to Kailasha was surprised to find a strange young boy outside Parvati's chamber. As he approached the door the boy moved, blocking his path. The Great God glared at him, anger rising.

'Step aside, boy,' he ordered. 'I wish to enter.'

The boy did not budge and Shiva's anger did not appear to bother him. 'No, you can't go in,' he said coolly.

'Move!' Shiva snapped. 'Now!' Who was this brat who dared to stop him, Shiva, from entering Parvati's chamber? His smouldering eyes bored into the boy.

'You can't go in,' the boy repeated. 'My mother said not to let anyone in.'

'I don't care what *your* mother said,' Shiva thundered. 'Now get out of my way!'

'No,' the boy said, looking fearlessly at the furious god who towered above him, snakes weaving, the crescent moon glowing an angry red.

When the boy refused to move, Shiva's rage exploded. He drew out his sword and cut the boy's head off with one clean stroke. As the sword touched his tender neck, the boy cried, 'Mother!' and Parvati came running out, but she was too late. She saw the head roll away and lie still.

Parvati turned on Shiva like a raging tigress, hot angry tears streaming down her cheeks. 'What

have you done?' she cried. 'You heartless brute, you killed my son! How could you? I'll never forgive you for this!'

'How was I to know he was your son?' Shiva asked reasonably, trying to calm his raging wife.

'You should have known!' Parvati cried. 'Some Great God you are!'

'I am sorry,' Shiva apologized quickly. 'Look, I'll restore him to life right away.'

Parvati shot him one burning look. Shiva thought of his attendants, the ganas, and they appeared. 'Bring me the head of the first living thing you see,' he commanded.

The ganas went out of Kailasha and the first living thing they saw was an old tusker ambling down a forest path. They cut its head off and gave it to the Great God. Shiva knelt down and placed the elephant's head on the raw, bleeding neck. The head joined seamlessly and the small eyes flickered and opened.

Shiva raised his son and embraced him. 'You, my son, will be the leader of my ganas and so will be known as Ganapati. No god or man will begin any venture without first making offerings to you. In you shall lie the power to remove all obstacles from the path of men and the wisdom of the ages.' Turning to Parvati he said, 'Happy now?' Her displeasure was the only thing he feared.

Parvati's eyes snapped dangerously and then a reluctant smile lit her face. Taking her son's hand she said, 'Come, I will take you to meet your brother Skanda. He commands the god's armies.'

As Parvati led Ganapati away Shiva meekly followed in their wake. 'That's a major crisis averted,' he thought, gazing fondly at the retreating backs of his wife and son.

How the bulbul became king of birds

• *Illustrated by Prerna Kathju* •

The great hornbill was once the king of the birds. He was as harsh as his voice and crueller than his hard beak. The fierce hawks and the big grey owls never felt his wrath, but the little ones knew all about it. It was them he picked on. Woe betide any little bird who made a mistake. He'd pin down the fluttering little creature with his heavy talons and, with a swift slash of his massive beak, tear the tiny thing open. The birds grew weary of his cruel ways and held a secret meeting in the branches of a great banyan tree.

'We must get another king,' said the grey-owl. 'The hornbill doesn't deserve to be king. He uses his power to attack the weak and helpless.'

'Let's make the peacock our king,' said the common pigeon who wished its feathers were not a dull grey. 'He is so beautiful and he has a readymade crown on his head.'

'No,' said the others, 'he's too vain and when the rains come he spends all his time dancing.'

'What about the goose?' said the sparrow.

'No,' said the rest. 'He comes only when the cool winds begin to blow. When the winds turn warm he'll fly to the north and leave us behind.'

And so it went on until the parrot said, 'I think the bulbul should be our king.'

'Hmm, that suggestion has some merit,' said the wise-looking stork. 'He sings sweetly, has a happy, cheerful nature and above all he is not cruel and vengeful.'

'He doesn't hurt tiny birds like me,' said the tailor-bird bobbing his tail.

'But who'll tell the hornbill he is no longer king?' asked the small blue kingfisher fearfully. 'He will kill the one who does.'

'I have an idea,' said the brown wood-owl. 'But I'll need your help,' he said to the woodpecker. In low whispers he told the birds his plan and all agreed it was excellent.

A few weeks later the brown-owl went to the hornbill who was sitting on a peepal tree, preening his feathers.

'Why are you here?' asked the hornbill. 'Aren't you supposed to be asleep?'

'Your majesty, the birds want to put you to a test, just to remind themselves how worthy you are,' the owl said with a bow. 'And when you pass everyone will know you are the rightful king of the birds.'

The hornbill thought and since thinking didn't come easily to him, he took a while. 'Very well,' he said at last, 'what do you want me to do?'

'You will have to fly up into the sky, land on a thick branch and break it. Whoever does that will be king of birds,' the owl told him, adding silkily, 'you have no serious competition, you're bound to win.'

They flew to a clearing where the birds were all gathered. 'Which branch do you want me to break?' asked the hornbill. 'Hurry up, I don't have all day.'

'That one,' said the owl pointing to a thick branch on a huge silk-cotton tree.

The hornbill flew up and landed on the branch as heavily as he could but the branch didn't even stir. He jumped on it, thumping hard but there was not so much as a crack. The hornbill looked down at his subjects in a right royal temper. 'If I can't break it, no one can, so I'm still king!' he shouted, glaring at them with his cruel eyes.

'We want the bulbul to try, your majesty,' chorused the birds, undaunted.

'That puny little tweeter!' sneered the hornbill with his beak in the air. 'Let him try, but mind, the branch must be as thick as this one.'

The owl pointed to another branch, even thicker than the one he was perched on. 'Is that thick enough, your majesty?' he asked.

'Yes,' said the hornbill with a rude laugh. 'Let me see him break that!'

The bulbul rose into the air filling the clearing with his melodious song and then darting down, he landed on the branch with a flutter of his wings. C-c-r-r-a-a-c-k went the branch and crashed to the ground. The hornbill was so surprised it fell off its perch and landed in the thorny branches.

The birds in the trees twittered and cheeped and cooed and hooted. 'The bulbul shall be our king! Long live the bulbul!'

The hornbill climbed out of the tangled branches, glared at his former subjects balefully and flew away. As soon as he was out of sight the birds began to laugh.

'Did you see his face?' asked the parrot giggling. 'The fool didn't know that the woodpecker had bored through the branch. A feather would have broken it! That was a very good idea, owl.'

And so the bulbul became the king of the birds and his subjects were very happy with their choice. Though it must be added that not all creatures choose their kings so wisely or so well.

The warrior goddess

• Illustrated by Ajanta Guhathakurta •

Mahisha, the mighty king of the asuras, became the most powerful man in all the three worlds because of a boon granted to his father. Neither god nor asura could kill him. Drunk with power and pride, Mahisha unleashed a reign of terror. He killed the king of Yakshas and took over their world and then he turned his eyes on Devaloka, the abode of the gods. The gods fought valiantly but were no match for Mahisha when he took on the form of a ferocious buffalo. His great horns could tear off mountain peaks and his pawing hooves could crack the heavens open.

Mahisha threw the gods out of their heavens and plunged the world into darkness and chaos. The light went out of the sun and the moon lost its glow; the wind lost its fleetness and the fire lost its heat; the clouds lost their raindrops and the rainbow disappeared. For the gods who governed them had gone.

The gods fled to Brahma, Vishnu and Shiva. 'You must help us destroy Mahisha,' they pleaded.

'We can't help you,' Shiva said, looking grave. 'You forget the boon—no god can slay him. That means not even I.'

'There must be a way to get around this boon,' said Indra thoughtfully.

'We'll have to wait until Time gets him,' Brahma said wearily. 'I should never have granted his father that boon.'

Vishnu, who was absently twirling his chakra, suddenly began to smile and the gods gave him a sour look. There was nothing funny about their situation.

'There is a way out,' Vishnu said, his smile getting wider. 'The boon says no god or asura may kill him, but says nothing about a goddess.'

Brahma and Shiva quickly caught his drift. 'This notion is sheer genius!' Shiva applauded.

'Isn't it?' said Vishnu sweetly.

'What notion?' asked Indra a little testily.

'You will see,' Shiva replied mysteriously. 'Now each one of us must release a portion of the power within us.'

From every godly forehead, a flickering flame of light released itself and floated out. The flames of light then merged and became one glowing radiance, and in the centre of that divine brightness was a formless being. The gods gave it form. Yama gave his long, curling hair, Shiva gave his face, Vishnu his arms and Brahma gave the being feet. All the gods contributed. The wind god gave ears, Indra gave the waist, and when all was done, a female figure emerged and stood before the gods—a woman of heavenly beauty with the grace and the glory of the gods. Kubera, the god of wealth, covered her with jewels and Himavat gave her a lion for her steed. Then each god gave her his personal weapon and when she was fully armed, she said, 'I am born to wage war on your enemies, but no god will assist me. Now tell me whom you want me to destroy.'

'You must kill Mahisha, king of the asuras,' Shiva said.

Durga, as she was called, sat on her lion and rode to Mahisha's palace. Mahisha heard a challenging battle cry and came out. Before him stood no fierce warrior but a woman of incredible beauty—perfect down to her dainty feet. Mahisha gazed at her and lost his heart. 'Why do you want to fight me, lovely one?' he asked. 'Marry me instead and rule all the three worlds.'

'Defeat me in battle and I'll marry you,' came the reply in sweet dulcet tones.

Mahisha laughed into her smiling yes. 'You're as fragile as the wind-flowers that bloom in the mountains, soft and beautiful. The weapons you bear seem too heavy for your slender arms. Give up this idea of fighting me. Even the mighty gods can't defeat me, how will you? They are not even here to assist you,' he said with a sneering laugh. 'Why?'

'Because I don't need them,' Durga said softly. 'I challenge you again. Are you afraid to fight me?'

Mahisha laughed. 'All right, I will fight you and when I have defeated you, I will marry you.'

The battle between the goddess and the asura was the most terrible the world had ever seen. Mahisha first sent out his champions but Durga killed them with insulting ease. The asura then came out himself—armed to the teeth. They clashed with a deafening roar and Mahisha abruptly changed into a mighty buffalo. The hot air from his nostrils burnt everything around and his great hooves cracked the earth. As he charged, trying to gore her with his horns, Durga rose and struck him with Shiva's trident. He pawed the ground, roaring with anger, crumbling hills into fine dust. Durga then whirled her lasso and caught his head in the noose. As she drew the rope in, the raging beast shook the heavens and the earth. Durga dragged Mahisha to her and leaping down from the lion placed her foot on his neck and cut his head off even as he was changing his form back to his own. And all the while the goddess smiled. When his twitching form grew still, fire got back its heat, the moon its glow, the sun its glory and the wind its might.

'Victory to Mahadevi!' the gods cheered. 'Victory to the great goddess!'

Walking on water

• *Illustrated by Bindia Thapar* •

An old sage was once meditating on the bank of a river. Another sage, standing across him on the other bank saw him and, as he was stuffed with his own worth, decided to show the old sage a thing or two. He raised his hands and chanting a mantra glided smoothly on the water and stepped ashore bang in front of the old man. He stood looking down at him waiting for an exclamation of admiration. But the old sage said nothing.

'Didn't you see what I just did?' he asked irritably.

'I did,' the old man said mildly. 'I saw you walking on the water. What did it take to do that?' he asked curiously.

'Twelve long years of the most painful and difficult penances,' the young sage said proudly. 'In the high reaches of the Himalayas, I stood in the eternal snows on one leg and ate only once a week.'

But the old sage was quite unimpressed. 'Oh dear, such a silly thing to do, all those terrible ordeals,' he remarked. 'Our ferryman would have rowed you across for just a couple of rupees.'

Savitri and Satyavan

• Illustrated by Avishek Sen •

The land of Madra was once ruled by Ashvapati and his queen Malati. They had everything they could possibly want except their heart's desire—they had no children. The sorrowing king and queen found no joy in anything and with time they grew old. But though past his prime, the king was determined to have a son. He went into the forest and prayed to the goddess Savitri, sister of the sun god. After years of prayer and penance Savitri appeared to the old king. 'What do you want?' the goddess asked.

'Grant me sons,' said the king, 'for life is empty without them.'

'Sons you shall not have,' said the goddess, 'but you shall have a daughter of great wisdom and strength. She will bring you more fame than any son could.'

Satisfied, the king returned to his capital and nine months later the queen gave birth to a lovely baby girl. The girl had lustrous hair, black as night and skin like golden sunlight.

'We shall name her Savitri, in honour of the goddess,' the king decided.

Years passed and Savitri grew into a beautiful young woman, wise and noble as she was lovely. But when it was time for her to wed, not a single king came to ask for her hand. Everyone who saw her was so overwhelmed by her radiant beauty and virtue that they bowed to her as if she was a goddess, far above their touch. And so the days passed and Savitri remained unwed. And the king grew sad and worried.

One day, when the court was assembled, the king sent for Savitri. 'My dear child, it is time for you to marry. As no one has come to seek you, you must go out and seek a husband. The choice is yours, but choose well and bring no shame upon our name.'

The princess, accompanied by her father's trusted councillors, travelled across the length and breadth of the land and met many monarchs, but no one she wanted to marry. Weary of travelling, she told the councillors she wanted to go home. 'This journey is futile. Let's return. Perhaps it is my fate not to wed.'

On the way back they were passing through a forest, lush and blooming, when she spied a young man near the forest track. On his back was a bundle of firewood and the bag on his shoulder was filled with fruits and flowers. But he walked like a king and his face had a serene beauty that no hardship could mar. Savitri looked at the noble young face and knew her search had ended. 'Stop,' she cried to the charioteer. 'Stop, please.'

The chariot came to a halt and Savitri asked her old advisor to find out who the young man was.

The advisor stepped down from the chariot and walked up to the young man, who bowed respectfully to him. 'He does just as he should,' Savitri thought happily. She saw the two men exchange words and then the young man bowed and walked away.

'Who is he?' Savitri asked her advisor when he returned.

The old man smiled at her. 'You have chosen well, princess. He is Satyavan, son of the blind king Dyumatsena, King of Salva.'

'Then why is he in the forest living like a hermit?' she asked, puzzled.

'The story is a sad one,' the advisor said heavily. 'Not long after Satyavan was born, the king went blind and the throne was usurped by his enemies. The blind king, the queen and their son were forced to live in the forests, suffering hardship and poverty. The prince looks after his old parents with tender care. That, he says, is his highest duty.'

'That is all I need to knew about him,' Savitri said softly.

She returned to her father's kingdom and went straight to the court where she found her father sitting with Narada, the celestial wandering rishi. She bowed to him.

'Where are you coming from?' asked the rishi.

'My father sent me to find a husband, holy one,' Savitri replied frankly.

'And have you?' he asked, his eyes twinkling.

'Yes, holy one, I have,' came the soft but firm answer.

The king beamed happily when he heard that. At last he would see his beloved daughter wed. 'Whom have you chosen?' he asked with a fond look.

'Satyavan, son of King Dyumatsena,' Savitri said and a hush fell on the court.

The king's pleasure died abruptly. 'You can't marry him!' he exclaimed in dismay. 'His father has no kingdom... they live like forest-dwellers.'

'Your daughter has chosen the finest in the land,' Narada told the agitated king. 'The prince is wise and good. He is absolutely truthful, never lies even in jest and that is why he is known as Satyavan. He has another name, the Horse Painter, for he can paint horses with the wind in their manes and thunder in their hooves. And above all he is a dutiful son who cares for his old parents without complaint. Such is the man your daughter has chosen, and she has chosen well indeed.'

The king looked happier but Narada's next words brought the gloom back. 'There is one problem though. He is fated to die exactly one year from today.'

The king looked sadly at his daughter. 'Choose someone else, my child. You can't marry him. In a year these eyes of mine will see you in widow's weeds, and that I will not be able to bear. Choose another.'

'No father, my choice is made,' Savitri said quietly. 'If I can't marry him, I won't marry at all. I'd rather be Satyavan's widow than a lesser man's wife.'

Narada clapped. 'Bravo!' he cried. 'You have the courage and nobility of a goddess! I approve of your choice.'

If the rishi approved, the king naturally had to do so too. Narada blessed Savitri and left. Preparations for the wedding were made and the king accompanied by his councillors took Savitri to the forest. When they reached the hermitage the king stepped down and went in. He found the old, blind king sitting under an enormous sal tree on a bed of kusa grass. The two kings greeted each other and when civilities were over, Savitri's father told the blind king why they had come.

'I am here to offer you my daughter,' he said.

The blind king looked unhappy. 'She has been brought up in a palace and will hanker for its comforts. She will not be able to live the harsh life of a forest-dweller.'

'My daughter has been well taught,' King Ashvapati said proudly. 'She knows happiness and sorrow are both fleeting as are pleasure and pain and she regards both equally. She can live in the forest with as much ease as she can in a palace.'

At that the blind king's face lit up. The sages and the rishis who lived in the forest were invited and Savitri and Satyavan were married. As soon as her father left, Savitri took off her silken robes and jewels and put on coarse garments dyed red with the juice of flowers. She took over Satyavan's duties and looked after the old king and queen. She fed them, bathed them, combed their hair and did all that was needed for their comfort and the old couple blessed the day she came into their lives.

Savitri went about her work cheerfully, hiding her great sorrow deep within her heart. No one could tell that she watched Death draw nearer and nearer her beloved husband with each passing day. When only three days of his life remained Savitri began to fast.

'There is no need for you to fast, my dear,' the blind king said. 'You are a good and kind child.'

'Why are you fasting?' the queen asked. 'Why a complete fast, without even water?'

'It's only for three days,' Savitri said evading the question. She couldn't possibly tell the old king and queen what she knew. It would kill them and so she bore her sorrow all alone.

On the last day of Satyavan's life Savitri decided to accompany her husband into the forest. 'It's a long hard walk and you're weak with fasting,' Satyavan protested. 'Stay back, I'll take you another day.'

'I want to be with you today,' Savitri said. 'The forest is blooming and filled

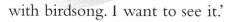

with birdsong. I want to see it.'

'Take her with you,' the blind king told his son. 'She hasn't left the hermitage since she came here.'

Savitri and Satyavan walked through the woods where peacocks danced among the flower-decked trees and bees hummed and sang as they gathered pollen and nectar. But Savitri's eyes were on her husband and the beauty went unnoticed. 'My eyes, you will not see him after this day, so look your fill,' she thought.

As they walked Satyavan filled his cloth-bag with berries and fruit, and when they came to a shady grove he said, 'You rest while I chop some wood.'

The day was warm and Savitri leaned against the broad trunk of a tree, her eyes fixed on her husband. The axe swung rhythmically and the pile of wood began to grow. Then suddenly perspiration began to stream down his face and body and the axe now moved slowly. 'So the time has come,' Savitri thought, showing no sign of her unbearable pain.

The axe dropped out of Satyavan's limp hand and he said, 'I feel so terribly tired, Savitri. My limbs feel numb and my head feels like it is being pierced by a thousand darts. Let me rest my head in your lap.'

Savitri rose quickly and caught his slack form as it fell. She sat there, with her husband's head in her lap. 'Death is coming to take my beloved lord,' she thought, feeling the clammy skin, 'and there is nothing I can do to stop him.' She neither wept nor cried, just held her sorrow close, waiting for the taker of souls. Suddenly the air began to shimmer and from the shimmering light a man emerged. He was as tall as the giant trees and glowed like the sun. His garments were redder than blood and rays of light shot out from the jewelled crown on his head. What frightened Savitri was the noose he held in his hand, but she looked at him calmly. Gently she placed Satyavan's head on the soft green grass and rose, bowing with palms folded. 'You come from the Lord of Death,' she said, her voice trembling slightly.

'I am Yama himself,' the bright being said. 'I'm here for your husband's soul.'

Savitri was a little surprised but not afraid. 'Lord, you usually send your emissary. Why have you come personally?'

'When a high-souled person dies I come myself; it would be an insult to send anyone else,' Yama told her as his shining noose snaked over Satyavan's still form. As he drew it in, Satyavan's soul, hardly bigger than a thumb, lay in the coils. His purpose fulfilled, Yama turned and walked away.

But as the god strode through the trees he heard the soft tread of bare feet on leaves behind him. Turning around he saw Savitri following in his steps.

'You cannot come where I go, Savitri,' he said gently. 'Go back and arrange your husband's funeral.'

'God of death, you are also god of dharma. You should know better than anyone else that a wife must follow her husband,' Savitri pointed out. 'And so I must follow you.'

Yama was pleased. 'I like what you say. Ask for anything except your husband's life and I will grant it.'

'Grant that his father, the blind king, may see again,' Savitri said, without pausing to think.

'So be it,' Yama said and walked on.

But the footsteps still followed. 'You must return,' the god said firmly. 'You cannot come with me.'

'Lord, the wise say if you walk seven steps with a stranger, the stranger becomes a friend and I have walked more than seven steps with you.' Yama's lips twitched but his face remained stern. 'And so, bearing that friendship in mind, I take the liberty of asking you, how can I not follow as a good wife should?'

Yama realized this was no ordinary woman. Pleased by her wisdom and insight he granted her another boon, anything except her husband's life.

'Grant that my husband's father regain his kingdom,' Savitri said.

'So be it, now go back,' Yama said, pleased that she asked nothing for herself.

But Savitri followed and Yama told her to turn back as she must be tired. 'You have been fasting and I have a long way to go.'

'How can I be tired when I'm following my husband?' she asked. 'How can I feel fatigue?'

Pleased, Yama granted her yet another boon. 'Not your husband's life, mind,' he said.

'Grant my father can have a hundred sons,' Savitri said. 'He has always longed for sons.'

Yama granted it. 'You ask nothing for yourself and that pleases me greatly. Ask for something for yourself.'

Savitri lowered her eyes. 'Grant that I may have a hundred sons,' she said softly.

'So be it,' Yama said. 'Now you really must go back.'

But Savitri followed him and the god turned around and said irritably, 'I've granted you all you asked for. Now what do you want?'

'I don't mean to be rude, lord, but how can I have a hundred sons when you have my husband?' she asked with deceptive meekness. 'And if I don't have sons, your words, god of dharma, will be a lie.'

For a brief moment the god of death and dharma looked stupefied and then the forest rang with his amused laughter. 'You are a formidable lady, that was a neat trap you set!' he said. 'Your courage and presence of mind have gained you the impossible.' He untied the shining noose and the tiny soul was released. 'Satyavan will be a great king and will live for four hundred years,' he pronounced and vanished.

Savitri ran back to where Satyavan lay and crouched beside him. His grey face now had colour and breath moved in his chest. A tear fell on it and Savitri wiped it away. Satyavan's eyes opened and he sat up. 'What happened? As I fell asleep I thought I saw a great being dressed in red standing before me. Was that a dream?' Savitri helped him up.

'That was Yama, come to take your soul,' she said and briefly told him what had happened.

Satyavan look at his lovely wife in admiration. 'You have no peer,' he said. 'Never will any man have such a wife as you.'

It was getting dark. 'Come, we must go back to the hermitage. Your parents will be worried,' Savitri said picking up his axe.

All that Yama promised came to pass. Satyavan's father got his sight and his kingdom back. When he died, Satyavan became king and he lived happily with his beloved wife for a very long time and, as Yama had promised, they had a hundred sons.

Ganapati and the god of wealth

• Illustrated by Tapas Guha •

Ganapati loved good food above all other things and, fortunately for him, offerings of delicious dainties poured in all the time. For gods and men are always beginning some venture or another and pray to him before doing so. Kubera, the god of wealth, was extremely proud of his riches. No one, least of all Kubera himself, knew how much wealth he had. He was very generous with his wealth and he knew it. Gods and men sang his praises and Kubera loved that. 'I am rich and generous and praised by all,' he thought, mightily pleased with himself. 'I think I shall hold a banquet and invite all the gods and kings so that Shiva can see how great I am. And the others will be so impressed when they see that the chief guest is Shiva himself.' He lay back in his golden bed basking in his own glory.

The next day the cooks and housekeepers were set to work. His great hall, which was a hundred miles long and a hundred miles wide, was made of ivory, gold and lapis lazuli and decorated with rare flowers. Precious incense from the five wish-fulfilling trees wafted in the air and the couches were covered with cloth-of-gold. Invitations were sent to the gods and kings and when all was ready Kubera went to Kailasha. He bowed before Shiva who was sitting with Parvati and their two sons. 'Lord, I've come to invite you and your family to a banquet. All the important gods and kings will be there. As you know, great one, I am very generous with my wealth and I am loved by all, so no one will refuse.'

At this, Shiva's brow rose a fraction of an inch. 'I am honoured, Kubera, but I cannot come, I have much to do here,' he said with a smile. He knew quite well why he was being invited. Kubera had always been a silly show-off.

Flustered and disappointed Kubera fell at Shiva's feet. 'Oh Lord, if you don't come, I will lose face!' he cried. 'I've told everyone you are going to be the guest of honour. If you can't come let Devi and the children attend the feast.'

'I attend no feast without my lord,' Parvati said, taking her cue from Shiva. Also, she disliked tasteless displays of wealth and with Kubera it was always too much of everything.

'I'm sorry, I can't attend either,' Skanda said rising. 'I have to deal with some asuras.'

Kubera's face fell. His name would be in the mud now. 'Oh lord, what will I do now?' he moaned.

Shiva glanced at his little son Ganapati and a smile crinkled his eyes. Kubera needed a lesson. 'Well I think my little one is not too busy to attend,' he said. 'And he does love a good feast.'

Kubera was greatly relieved. He took Ganapati to his palace. All the gods and kings were in the fabulous banquet hall. The plates and serving dishes were made of gold and winking gems encrusted the golden goblets. Even the finger-bowls were rimmed with rare pearls and the massive tables groaned under the weight of the food. Kubera surveyed the scene and his breast swelled with pride and satisfaction. 'Come and sit down,' he said to the little god, leading him to a golden throne covered with rubies and diamonds. Ganapati plonked on the cushion and said, 'I'm hungry. I want to eat.'

Kubera clapped and half-a-dozen attendants rushed to serve the little god. The other guests waited, as was proper. They would eat when Shiva's son was done.

Ganapati ate and he ate and he ate. Dishes emptied faster than they could be filled.

'How much can he eat?' Kubera wondered in dismay as he viewed the empty vessels. He had other guests to feed too but that did not seem to weigh with the little god. He ate steadily until there was not a crumb left on the table. 'I am still hungry,' Ganapati said petulantly. 'I want more food.'

Panting cooks filled the dishes to the brim once more and Ganapati ate up all that was served. 'Is that all there is?' he asked pouting. 'I'm still hungry,' he told the stunned god of wealth who stood looking down at him with his jaw hanging loose.

'Bring more food,' Kubera said to the cooks.

'There's no more, my lord,' the cooks informed him. 'We will have to prepare some.'

'Then do so,' Kubera said tartly, with a wary eye on the little god who sat scowling on the throne.

The cooks rushed off to the kitchens and Ganapati jumped down and followed them. 'If the food is in the kitchen, I am going there,' he said to Kubera.

Ganapati went to the kitchen and ate up all the half-cooked food as well as the raw stuff. Then he went to the pantry and ate whatever he could find there. When it stood nice and empty he went to Kubera's treasury and began eating the pearls and gold and gems.

The god of wealth saw his boundless treasure

dwindling before his eyes until all that remained were a couple of pearls in the corner. Kubera could have cried in anguish. His treasury had never stood empty!

'I am still hungry,' Ganapati said irritably to the dazed god. Then Kubera noticed the little god looking at him with a wicked gleam in his eyes. 'Since there's nothing left to eat, I think I'll eat you!'

Kubera fled with the little god close behind. He ran to Shiva and fell at his feet, quivering with fear. 'Save me, lord, save me!' he cried. 'Your son has eaten me out of house and hearth and now he wants to eat me!'

Shiva's lips twitched. 'Didn't my little son get enough to eat at your feast?' he asked blandly. 'I would have thought you'd have a great spread at your banquet, you are the god of riches after all.'

'What riches? What banquet?' groaned Kubera, 'Your son ate up everything I have—my food, my treasure, and now he wants to eat me!'

Ganapati came running in and Shiva raised his hand. 'Well, my son, did you eat your fill?' he asked with a sweet smile that made Kubera wince.

'No,' grumbled the little pot-bellied god, 'I am still hungry and I'm going to eat him up, crown and all.'

Kubera trembled, clutching Shiva's tiger skin and Shiva almost laughed out loud. 'Go to your mother,' he said to his son. They smiled at each other mischievously and Kubera, glancing up, saw their smiles and realized he had been guilty of pride and vanity. 'Forgive me, lord, for my pride in my wealth. I had forgotten that it is you who gave it to me.'

Ganapati, standing behind his mother, poked his head out and grinned wickedly at him. Kubera cast one fearful look at the little god and scooted back to his palace. 'He looked at me as if I was a piece of roast venison!' thought the god as he bolted the door.

The welsher

• *Illustrated by Bindulika Sharma* •

One morning, Gopal, the barber of Krishnanagar, went to visit an old friend. He found him curled up on his bed, moaning and groaning in agony.

'What's the matter?' Gopal asked concerned.

'It's my stomach,' said the friend. 'Lord, does it hurt!'

'Have you seen the doctor?' asked Gopal.

'Yes, and much good his medicines are doing me,' the man grumbled. 'Waste of time, these doctors!'

Gopal looked at his miserable friend in pity. 'Try praying to Ma Kali,' he suggested. 'Offer her as much as your stomachache's worth and she'll cure you in a trice.'

'Give me some sensible advice if you have it,' the friend said sourly.

'I'm serious,' said Gopal. 'Just try it, it can't hurt more than it already does.'

The friend closed his eyes and prayed to Kali. 'Ma, if you make this pain go away I'll sacrifice a...a buffalo to you.' This stomachache was worth a buffalo, he thought as he lay back. In a few moments he sat up, looking surprised. 'Gopal, I'm already feeling better,' he said in wonder. 'Ma Kali is great!'

'Good. In that case you'd better go and buy that buffalo,' Gopal said.

'A buffalo! No, no, this is just a niggling pain,' the friend said. 'A goat should be enough.'

'Well, buy the goat then. I hope, for your sake, Ma Kali understands,' Gopal told him with a disapproving look.

The friend stood up, wiggled his feet and walked around the room. 'I'm ever so much better,' he declared, adding slyly, 'I think a chicken should be enough. There's hardly any pain.'

'Be careful,' Gopal warned, 'you are pushing your luck too far.'

But the friend was striding up and down, his mind working on other lines. 'What will Ma Kali do with a chicken. She would probably prefer a sparrow and since I can't catch it, I'm sure she will catch it herself,' the cunning fellow said.

'*You'll catch it now*,' Gopal said, 'trying to outsmart Ma Kali!'

Even as he spoke his friend collapsed on the floor, holding his stomach and screaming in agony.

'Serves you right,' Gopal said severely. 'Now you'd better apologize to Ma Kali and offer her what your stomachache is worth.'

'O Ma Kali, make me well,' the man wailed. 'I promise I'll sacrifice a buffalo.' But the pain remained. 'I'll give you two buffaloes.' The pain stayed put. 'I'll give you—three—four—five buffaloes,' he said wincing in pain at the thought of all those buffaloes he would have to buy. That hurt almost as much as his stomachache.

As he said 'five' the pain began to fade away and soon was gone.

'Buy the buffaloes now,' advised Gopal, adding wickedly, 'and buy a goat and chicken too. You don't want to annoy Ma Kali, do you?'

The friend looked doubtfully at Gopal, who looked back innocently at him. Then with a disgusted look he went to the market to buy the beasts and fowl. He'd buy the lot and take no chances, though he was certain he'd been had by Gopal.

Gopal laughed gleefully when his friend left.

'Thanks to me, Ma Kali, today you get a bonus.'

The snake in the prince's belly

• *Illustrated by Suddhasattwa Basu* •

There once lived a king named Devashakti who ruled over a great kingdom. He had only one sorrow in life and that was his son. The prince was slowly wasting away because a snake was living in his stomach. Magicians and doctors were called but no magic or medicine could rid the prince of the snake. And the prince continued to shrivel like a drying gourd.

The poor prince was sad and weary but his parents' sorrow hurt him the most. So he decided to leave home and go as far away as he could. Months later, he reached a big city and walking around came across a large temple. 'I'll live here and beg for alms,' the prince thought as he sat on the steps.

Now the king of this kingdom was called Bali and he had two beautiful daughters. Every morning the princesses greeted their father, each in her own way.

'May the king be forever victorious,' the elder princess always said with much drama.

'O, king, may you receive your just deserts,' the younger princess said simply.

This went on day after day and the younger daughter's greeting began to irritate the king. It sounded rude and critical.

One morning, when the younger princess greeted him, the king's rage boiled over.

'Guards! Ministers!' he shouted. 'Take her away from my sight! Her words are jarring to the ear! Marry her off to some

outsider and let *her* get her just deserts!'

The ministers felt sorry for the princess but they had to obey the king. The princess, however, was unmoved by the king's command. Accompanied by a few maids, she went with the king's men out of the palace and into the world.

They walked through the city until they came to a big temple. There the ministers saw a young beggar who appeared to have come from another land and, as commanded by the king, they married the princess to him. The princess married him without one word of complaint. In fact she married the sickly beggar quite happily, and when he decided to travel to another land, she went with him.

After many days of travelling they came to a fine city. There they found a little house built on the edge of a pond and made it their home. The princess looked after her husband lovingly, taking care of all his needs.

One day, leaving her sick husband at home, she went to the market with her maids. When she returned, she found her husband sleeping outside, his head resting against a huge anthill. Then to her horror, out of his half-open mouth appeared the head of a snake. It spread out its hood swaying from side to side. A moment later, out of the anthill came another hooded snake.

When the snakes spied each other, they hissed and spat angrily. The anthill snake said, 'You wicked creature! How can you torment the poor prince by living in his stomach?'

The princess was surprised. 'So my husband is a prince!' she thought happily.

The snake in the prince's mouth hissed. 'You're no better. You sit on two pots of gold and kill those who try to take it! You're a nasty piece of work.'

The snakes fought, darting and spitting venom, and their secret weaknesses came out into the open. And the princess heard it all.

'You worm! It's so easy to kill you,' the anthill snake hissed. 'All one has to do is give the prince a drink made from black mustard seeds and you'll be dead!'

'Hah!' spat the snake in the prince's mouth. 'It's even simpler to get rid of you. All one has to do is pour a pot of boiling oil or water into the anthill and you'll join your forefathers!'

The princess waited quietly until the two snakes returned to their homes. Then she woke up her husband and gave him a drink made of black mustard seeds and the snake in his belly died. Next, she poured boiling oil into the anthill and killing that snake, dug up the two pots of gold.

'Now my lord, we will return to my father's palace,' she said.

The king was sitting on his throne when he saw his daughter walk in, dressed in jewels and silks! And with her was no beggar but a young prince.

'I've received my just deserts,' she said quietly to her father.

The king looked down in shame, for now he realized that everyone does get their just deserts. He welcomed his daughter with tears of joy.

'Yes, my dear, you have,' he said. 'Though I married you to a beggar, you have come back with a prince. I sent you away poor and you return rich.'

The snakes, the princess and the king, all received their just deserts.

Arjuna wins Draupadi

• *Illustrated by Arvinder Chawla* •

After Bhima killed Vakasura, life in Ekachakra resumed its placid pace. The Pandavas lived quietly, avoiding any attention. One evening, a stranger arrived at their door and Kunti offered him food and shelter for the night. Over dinner he told the Pandavas that Draupada, King of Panchala, was holding a swayamvara for his daughter Draupadi.

'The fire-born princess is more beautiful than a blue lotus beaded with dew,' the man said. 'That flawless beauty will bring all the monarchs of the land to Panchala. Lucky will be the man who wins her.'

He went on to describe Draupadi's beauty at great length and the five young men paid attention as they never had before. He told them how she was born out of the sacrificial fire, emerging full-born from the flames. 'The king performed the sacrifice to obtain a son and got the princess as a bonus.'

That night sleep deserted the five brothers. All each one could think of was the princess whose dark beauty made senses reel. The next morning they told their mother that it was time to leave Ekachakra and move on.

'We've been here too long,' Yudhishthira said.

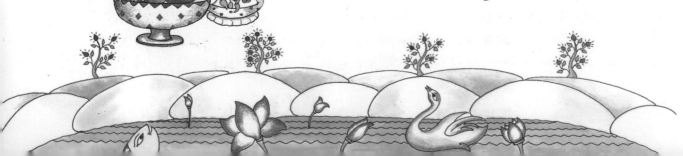

'Duryodhana's spies are in the city,' Arjuna added. 'If they spot Bhima, all is lost.'

All her sons gave her excellent reasons to leave. Kunti looked at their feverish sleepless eyes and hid her smile. 'My sons are smitten,' she thought with a silent laugh. 'Very well, if that's what you want, my sons. I think we ought to go to Panchala,' she suggested in bland tones. 'We've never been there and I hear it is a beautiful city.'

'We will do as you say, mother,' Yudhishthira said quickly.

'As we always do,' the rest chorused.

They packed their meagre belongings, thanked their kind host and left. The highway to Panchala was filled with jostling crowds, all in a holiday mood. They were going to see the great celebrations and perhaps catch a glimpse of the lovely princess. Once in the city they found lodgings in the house of a poor potter. The Kauravas too were in the city but Duryodhana's spies would never think to search the poorer quarters—not that they would have recognized the princes anyway. A year of running and hiding had altered the Pandavas greatly. And Bhima's imposing bulk was hidden under a loosely draped shawl.

King Draupada stood at the window and looked sourly at the royals thronging the palace grounds. 'I always wanted Draupadi to marry Arjuna, Pandu's son,' he thought. 'And it would have been but for that ill-begotten Duryodhana! Murdered Queen Kunti and the boys. But no airy-fairy king is going to wed my daughter! They'll have to compete for her and only one as good as Arjuna will win her.'

The morning saw the great amphitheatre filled with spectators and suitors. The commoners sat on one side, the brahmins on the other and in the centre sat the kings on golden thrones. Among them were Duryodhana and his brothers, Karna, Krishna and his brother Balarama, and Jarasandha, Emperor of Magadha. The Pandavas entered and sat quietly among the brahmins. They looked no different with their matted topknots and coarse bark clothes and nobody except Krishna noticed that there was something different about the five young men. Unlike the rest, these five had hard-muscled bodies and they held themselves like princes. He whispered something in Balarama's ear and the latter swiftly surveyed the brahmin enclosure. 'You're right, they could be our cousins. So they escaped the fire. Duryodhana will be mad as a bull when he finds out, and a little afraid I think,' Balarama said, looking at the Kauravas with active dislike.

The activities in the arena claimed their attention and ended the conversation. A strange mechanical contraption was rolled into the centre and against it was a great long bow—unstrung. The princess entered, escorted by her brother, and the chatter died swiftly as the suitors gazed ardently at her and grimly at each other. The Prince of Panchala raised a hand. 'Listen carefully, you monarchs,' he said in a voice that carried to the last row. 'You see the ring on the pole fixed to the revolving wheel, and this bow here? Behind the ring lies the target. If you wish to win my sister, you must string this bow, which is only a little smaller than Shiva's, shoot five arrows through the ring and bring the target down.'

The kings grew tense; this was not going to be easy. One by one they rose and tried to bend the bow but not one of them could even string it.

Arjuna looked at the bow and itched to get his hands on it, but he hadn't come there to compete. He watched the kings try and fail and with each failure the archer in him longed to string the bow and bring the target down. When all the kings had tried and failed, Arjuna rose, with one desire only—to string the bow. He didn't hear his brothers hissing. 'Sit down! What do you think you're doing?! Do you want Duryodhana to see us?!'

Arjuna walked into the arena and picked up the great bow.

The kings burst into loud mocking laughter when they saw the lean, young bark-clad brahmin handling the bow. Very unobservant men they were and nobody with the exception of Krishna took note of the bowstring marks on both shoulders, the mark of the ambidextrous Arjuna, the only one known to shoot with both hands.

Arjuna looped the bowstring into the top nock and in one fluid movement bent the great bow and strung it. He raised the bow with graceful ease, placed the arrows on the bowstring and drew it back. Five arrows swiftly following one another flew through the ring and the target dropped to the ground.

The scornful laughter fizzled out like live coals in the rain and black, glowering scowls replaced it. The kshatriya kings had been bested by a book-learning brahmin stripling! Angry words rose in the royal enclosure but wild cheers greeted Arjuna from the brahmin quarter. In fury, the kings watched the Princess of Panchala walk towards the bark-clad brahmin.

Draupadi looked at the tall, handsome young man and her eyes glowed like lamps in a dark night. Shyly she placed the garland around his neck and Arjuna took her soft hand into his own hard, calloused one. At that the kings rose outraged. 'A swayamvara is for kshatriyas! Brahmins cannot compete!' they shouted. 'Release the princess!'

'There's no law against it!' the triumphant brahmins yelled back. 'It's simply a custom, that's all. You kshatriyas are jealous because a brahmin has beaten you on your on turf!'

'The Princess must choose another,' the kings insisted and when they saw that it was not going to happen, they rushed into the arena, fully intent on killing the young brahmin.

Bhima, seeing his brother under attack, flung back his over-cloth and leapt into the arena placing himself between Arjuna and the murderously angry kings. Yudhishthira and the twins were at his heels and the kings, suddenly confronted by five well-muscled brahmins, fell back, more in surprise than fear. These brahmins behaved like warriors! But there was little room for further thought. The big one was hurling kings around like they were cushions and the one who had won the princess was shooting arrows with such accuracy, that no serious damage was inflicted. Most of the arrows sank into the rear-ends of the silk-clad monarchs which made them even more furious. When the fight turned ugly, the brahmins in the stands leapt into the fray, brandishing their water-pots and staffs. A right royal battle followed—water-pots landed on crowned heads and wooden staves smartly struck the noble backs.

Then above the clangour and clamour, a clear, even voice rang out, 'The Princess of Panchala has been fairly won,' Krishna said coolly and a faint mocking smile appeared when he spied Duryodhana's sullen face. 'A brahmin may compete, there is no law against it, the kshatriyas simply made the custom their own. This fight is absurd and foolish.'

Muttering darkly, the frustrated kings sheathed their swords and trickled out of the amphitheatre. The Pandavas, with Draupadi in the centre, slipped away through the other exit before the monarchs could gather their thoughts and work out why five young brahmins possessed the skills of kshatriya warriors. Just the number could have told them a great deal, but they were too angry to think.

The Pandavas quickly made their way back to the potter's house. Kunti, busy with some chore, didn't turn around when her sons entered.

'Look at what I got for alms today, mother,' Arjuna said with a laugh.

'Share it equally among yourselves,' Kunti said and then turned to face them. Her eyes widened in dismay when she saw Draupadi beside Arjuna.

'Oh, what have I done!' she exclaimed. 'Yet what I have said cannot be taken back.'

Yudhishthira bowed. 'We will obey you as we have always done,' he assured her.

After a simple meal, they put out the lamps and went to sleep.

But somebody *had* followed the Pandavas home. The Prince of Panchala wanted to know who had won his sister and had followed the brahmins to the potter's house. When all was dark, he stealthily opened the door and went in. He looked at the sleeping forms, carefully examining each one, and as he looked an expression of shock and amazement crossed his face. There were five young men—all with the bodies of trained warriors. Of the five, one was extremely large, two were twins and one had bowstring marks on both shoulders. The lady sleeping near them looked more regal than any queen he had seen.

'One set of twins, one large, plus two. And with them a lady who looks likes their mother. All this adds up to only one thing—the Pandavas are not dead! A Pandava won my sister!' was the exultant thought.

The prince sneaked out and quickly returned to the palace and though it was late, he went straight to his father's chamber. The lamps were still burning and the king sat at a table twiddling a reed pen, looking grim. He looked up quickly when his son entered. 'Have you found out who won Draupadi?' he asked tersely.

'Yes—and take that frown off your face,' the prince said smiling. 'You have got what you wanted. That brahmin who won my sister is none other than Arjuna, King Pandu's third son. The Pandavas and their mother escaped the fire.'

The king jumped up, disbelief mingling with hope. 'Are you sure?' he asked tensely.

'Almost as certain as I am of my own identity,' the prince said. 'Look, add this—five young men, out of which two are twins and one extremely large. With them is a lady who resembles them and looks more noble than any queen I have encountered. What does that make?'

'The Pandavas and their mother Kunti,' the king answered automatically. Then he hugged his son in delight. 'Now I am a happy man. Tomorrow we will invite them to a banquet and the world shall know that my daughter was won by the worthiest prince in the land, Arjuna, son of Pandu.'

The ten fools

• *Illustrated by Rosy Rodrigues* •

Emperors are at best whimsical people and Akbar was no exception. One day he sent for Birbal and said, 'I'm usually surrounded by the wisest in the land. I don't meet any fools. Bring me the ten greatest fools in the city. I will give you one month to find them.'

'Ah! Absurdity at its finest,' Birbal thought ruefully, saying, 'Certainly, sire, I'll bring you ten fools, and I won't need a month.'

Birbal rode out of the palace into the city of Agra. Barely five minutes later, he saw a man riding a horse carrying a bundle of firewood on his head. Birbal's eyes widened in astonishment. 'My good man, why don't you place that load behind you, on the horse?' he asked.

'Huzur, my horse is old. It will be too much for him—my weight and the weight of the wood, so I'm carrying it for him,' the man explained.

'Strike one!' Birbal thought with a small smile. 'Come with me, and your horse won't have to carry another load ever again,' he said.

'O, certainly huzur,' the man said happily. They rode on and, cutting across a park, Birbal saw a man lying on a grassy mound with his arms in the air. Nearby, his horse grazed placidly. Birbal thought the man had suffered a stroke and quickly dismounted. But as soon as he touched the man's arms to raise him up, the man shrieked, 'Don't move my hands! Don't touch them!'

'I'm awfully sorry,' Birbal apologized. 'Do they hurt?'

'No, of course they don't,' the man said. 'It's just that my wife asked me to buy a pot this big,' he said indicating the distance between his palms. 'If you move my hands, I'll get the wrong size and then my wife will never let me hear the end of it. Can she scold!'

'This is a superb specimen,' Birbal thought as he helped him up without moving the man's arms. 'Put your hands down and come with me and I'll give you a full set of pots, from the smallest to the largest. When your wife sees them she'll be so pleased, she'll probably never scold again.'

'That is very kind of you, sir,' the man said with a pleased nod, dropping his arms.

As Birbal was about to put his foot into the stirrup, a maulvi, running hell for leather, charged right into him and knocked him down. Very annoyed Birbal sat up and the maulvi said, words rushing out at top speed, 'O dear, O dear, pardon me, huzur, but I just called the Azaan, the evening prayer, from the mosque and I wanted to see how far my voice goes. I was running after it and now I'll never know, you've gone and spoilt it,' the maulvi complained.

Birbal couldn't believe his ears. His scowl vanished. 'I didn't know our city possessed such a gem!' he thought as he rose, dusting himself. 'I'm very sorry to have ruined the chase,' he said to the maulvi. 'I'm sure you can follow your voice another day. Come with me today and I'll make it up to you. I'll give you two gold mohurs.'

The grumpy maulvi beamed. 'I'll be quite happy to go with you, huzur,' he said rubbing his hands.

Birbal took the three fools to his palace and told his servants to take care of them. 'Wait here till I return,' he said to the three men and left.

Birbal didn't have to go far in his search for fools. Strolling through a public park he came across two men brawling with no holds barred.

'Stop that!' Birbal ordered pulling them apart. 'You could seriously hurt each other. What are you fighting about?' he asked. 'Perhaps I can help.'

'Huzur! He's going to set his tiger on my buffalo,' one shouted, indignantly.

'And I will,' snarled the other.

'Where are these beasts of yours?' Birbal asked looking around.

'You will?' said the first, trying to reach across Birbal to punch the other. 'You'll see them if God appears and grants us each a boon.'

'And I will get a tiger!' cried the other.

'This can't be happening!' Birbal thought.

'See, that's his nasty plan,' bawled the first. 'He says if I ask for a buffalo, he'll ask for a tiger to eat it up.'

'Will too!' growled the other and they were both at each other's throats again.

'Stop that, you idiots! Stop, I say!' Birbal shouted. 'His tiger won't eat your buffalo!' Then clasping his head he groaned, 'O lord, what am I saying. This foolishness is catching!'

Sanity returned as Birbal heard a voice

behind him say, 'Huzur, what a fool you are to take these morons seriously.'

Turning around Birbal saw a man with a large, heavy clay pot on his head. 'A fool you are, sir, and if I lie may my blood flow like the oil in this pot!' the man said pompously, swinging the pot down. It shattered and the man stared blankly at the thick sluggish stream. Then he slapped his head. 'O my god! Look at what I've done! All my fine, pure oil seeping into the ground!' he all but wept.

Birbal shook his head in amazement. This one was a beauty! 'Don't weep over spilt oil,' Birbal said smiling faintly. 'Come with me and I'll replace it.'

The man's face brightened and Birbal took the three fools home and left them there.

'I must get away from them for a while. A leisurely walk will clear my head,' he thought to himself.

Dusk fell gently over the city and a golden moon climbed out of the river. Birbal strolling along the bank, came across a man bent over double, searching for something on the ground.

'What are you looking for?' Birbal asked.

'My ring, sir,' the man replied.

'Did it fall here, on the path?' asked Birbal.

'No, sir, it fell under that huge peepal tree, but there is more light here, you see,' came the explanation.

'And I thought I'd seen them all!' was Birbal's thought as he said, 'Come with me and I'll give you another ring.' This one was truly a delight!

'Yes, sir,' the man said straightening.

The two walked on and they saw a man scrabbling in a heap of sand.

'What on earth are you doing?' Birbal exclaimed.

'I hid my ring in this sand pile and now I can't find it,' the man said.

'You marked the spot, I suppose,' Birbal asked.

'Of course I did, sir, I'm not stupid,' the man replied huffily. 'There was a nice fluffy cloud in the sky directly above my head when I put the ring in. And now that wretched cloud has gone and I can't find my ring,' he moaned.

A chuckle escaped Birbal's lips. This is too good to be true! 'Come with me and I will replace it,' he said to the man.

'You will?!' he cried out happily. 'I'll come at once, sir.'

'Now I've got eight,' Birbal thought. 'Two more to go.' Then a thought struck him and he laughed out loud. 'I know just who they are.'

He took the two men home and told his servants to prepare rooms for the eight fools. 'They will stay the night. And find out what they want for dinner.'

The next morning, when all were assembled in court, Birbal entered, shepherding the eight fools in.

'Back so soon, Birbal?' the Emperor asked, looking in amusement at the motley group.

'That really shouldn't surprise you, sire,' Birbal said with a rueful smile. 'The world is filled with fools, and our fair city has more than its share.'

As Birbal related each man's tale, the Emperor guffawed with laughter. 'But there are only eight here,' Akbar said wiping his eyes which brimmed again with laughter. 'I distinctly remember saying ten.'

'But there are ten, sire,' Birbal said, his face deadpan.

'Where are the other two?' the Emperor asked, looking over the heads of the eight fools.

'One stands before you and the other sits before me,' Birbal said, smiling faintly.

'How dare you!' thundered the Emperor and the court held its breath.

'And, I may add, sire, we are the biggest fools of the lot,' Birbal said with a broad smile, 'You for setting such an absurd task, and I for carrying it out!'

A silence fell, the Emperor glowered. Then his eyes twinkled and the whole court burst into laughter. And the merriest laugh was the Emperor's.

God in his wisdom

• *Illustrated by Ludmilla Chakrabarty* •

In a broad beautiful valley ringed by mountains, where the air smelt like honey and the waters tasted like nectar, there lived a man who was satisfied with nothing. When the moon shone full and golden over the lake, the man wished that it was a sickle moon shining. If the day was warm and bright he thought it ought

to be cool and cloudy. If the jasmines were blooming he wished the roses were in full bloom and if his wife made kheer he wished it was halva. He was one grouchy, grumpy man because nothing ever pleased him.

One day when he was sitting under a walnut tree, sourly surveying the world, he spied a pumpkin creeper. 'O God,' he said, 'you are really quite foolish. You give this huge walnut tree small little nuts and you give that skinny, gangling pumpkin vine such enormous fleshy fruit. Now if you had made nuts the size of pumpkins for the tree, and pumpkins the size of nuts for the vine, you would have shown some sense. I would have bowed to your wisdom, but as it...Ouch! Ouch!' he screamed.

A small green walnut had fallen on his bald pate. 'Ooo-ow!' he murmured rubbing the sore spot.

Then he looked up into the sky and bowed touching his forehead to the ground. 'I am truly grateful, God, that you in your wisdom made walnuts the size they are,' he said fervently. 'Had that walnut been the size of a pumpkin, my skull would have been lying around in tiny little pieces. Never will I question your wisdom again.'

Indra cons Karna

• Illustrated by Tapas Guha •

Karna, son of Surya and Kunti, was brought up by a humble charioteer. When he grew up he studied under Parasurama, the greatest of all sage warriors, and acquired mastery over every weapon used by man. Later, due to fate and destiny, he became Duryodhana's most trusted friend and Duryodhana made him King of Anga. But the kshatriyas never considered Karna their equal; they thought him low-born. No one suspected he was the eldest brother of the Pandavas, god-born like them. Kunti had kept that secret much too well.

After the Pandavas married Draupadi, King Dhritarashtra divided the kingdom between his sons and the Pandavas, but the Pandavas got a raw deal. The king gave them the wild, arid wastelands that lay beyond the forests of Khandava. The Pandavas did not complain or protest. Instead, they went to work and erected the most magnificent city on earth and called it Indraprastha. Their palace was designed by Maya, the architect of the gods himself. When Duryodhana, ever envious and filled with bitter hate, visited the city he swore to wrest it from them. With the help of his father and his wicked uncle Shakuni, he tricked Yudhishthira into playing a game of dice and Yudhishthira lost everything—wealth, cattle and kingdom. He sent the Pandavas into exile for thirteen years. They were to live twelve years in a forest and the last in a city, without being discovered. At the end of the term the kingdom would be returned, but, if discovered, they would be exiled for another thirteen years. Duryodhana was sure his spies would find them long before that. But the Pandavas were not found and by the end of the thirteenth year everyone, gods and men, began to prepare for a great war. They knew that Duryodhana would refuse to return the Pandavas' kingdom and the Pandavas would fight to reclaim it.

Indra, Arjuna's father, naturally wanted victory for his son and he knew the biggest thorn in Arjuna's path was Karna. His skill was as great as Arjuna's and he had the added advantage of the celestial armour and earrings he was born with. With them he was invincible.

'If I deprive him of Surya's armour and earrings he will be no threat to my son. I must get them somehow,' thought Indra.

Indra was very good at devious plans and he came up with a beauty.

'All the world knows that Karna has sworn to give anything if asked, especially when he is praying to Surya. That is when I must strike. I will go when he is praying and ask for the armour and earrings. He will have to give them to me or break his oath and lose his fame as the greatest of all givers.'

Surya found out what Indra intended doing and took immediate steps to foil his plans. That night, when Karna lay dozing on his bed, Surya appeared before his son in the guise of a handsome brahmin.

'Beware of Indra, Karna. He wants Arjuna to win at all costs and that can only happen if you give him your armour and earrings. He is going to come to you tomorrow to ask for them. Whatever you do, don't give them to him,' Surya warned. 'Give him jewels and cattle, gold and kingdom but not these celestial objects which sprang out of the ocean-churned amrita. If you value your life, you will do as I say.'

'Who are you and why do you show me such kindness?' Karna asked. 'I know you are no brahmin. Are you a god?'

'I am Surya, he of the thousand rays to whom you pray every morning, and so you are very dear to me,' Surya said. He did not tell him that he was his father; the time for that had not yet come.

Karna bowed low with folded palms. 'This is my greatest happiness—to behold you. But I cannot do as you ask,' he said quietly but firmly. 'I have vowed to give anyone who asks when I pray to you and that includes Indra. I will not break my

oath, not even if it means death. I
cannot live without honour. When
Indra comes I will give him whatever
he asks for. And I will gain by the act,'
he said with a twisted smile. 'Indra
will double my honour and fame and
he, on the other hand, will forever
be known as a low-down
trickster. Few men can claim
they gave alms to a god.'

'You are my greatest devotee,
my son. Don't throw your life
away,' Surya urged. 'Don't give
him what he asks for.'

'I must,' Karna said with a
trace of sadness. 'And if it brings
death, so be it.'

Surya realized that no argument
would make Karna break his vow. His
pride in his son was laced with sorrow for he
knew the consequences of this action. 'If you must give away your armour and
earrings then ask for his weapon, the thunderbolt, in exchange,' Surya advised. 'It will
be of use to you in the war that is to come. But remember you will be able to use it
just once,' he warned, 'so use it only when the need is dire. My blessings on you, my
son,' he said and vanished.

The next morning when Karna stood facing east, praying to Surya, a skinny,
ragged brahmin came and stood before him.

'Give,' he said flatly. When a brahmin asked, all gave, kings and commoners alike.

Karna looked at the brahmin with a faint smile. 'What do you want?' he asked,
though he knew.

'The armour and earrings you were born with,' the scrawny brahmin said, eyeing
the objects with shrewd eyes.

'Strange to find a god begging,' Karna remarked. 'I know who you are and why you're here. Aren't you afraid of becoming the laughing stock of the three worlds? What will happen to your reputation if word gets around that you, a god, petitioned a mortal? And you're not asking for a trifle, you're asking for a great deal, in fact practically my life. How will you live with the shame of receiving so much?' he asked, trying to goad Indra into changing his mind.

Indra said nothing, just held his hand out. 'Very well,' said Karna. 'I will give you my armour and earrings but to save your face, give me your thunderbolt.'

Indra looked sharply at him. 'So, as I suspected, Surya has warned you and yet you give!' he exclaimed admiringly. 'You could have avoided this encounter had you wished. I don't know any man who would have behaved with such honour. I will give you my vajra but it will not kill the one you want it for. And as Surya must have told you, you can use it but once. After that it will return to me.'

Karna knew it was a bad bargain but he was no haggler. 'No matter,' he said calmly as he drew out his sword, testing the edge on his thumb. Then with sure, swift, clean strokes he cut the armour off his body, skinning it off like a butcher skins a beast. His face showed no sign of pain as his blood flowed down in thick sluggish streams. And as he gave the blood-soaked golden armour to Indra the gods came out to witness this magnificent act of courage and generosity. Scented flowers rained gently on his head and, stained red with his blood, fell to the ground. The sword was raised again and with two swift strokes Karna cut the dazzling earrings off his ear lobes. Indra received them, head bowed in shame, and the gods cried 'Foul'.

The god was ashamed but not ashamed enough to return the celestial objects. He bowed to Karna. 'For this act of generosity you will be known as the greatest giver of all time and the wounds on your body will heal immediately without leaving a scar.'

The god vanished and the red lips of Karna's wounds slowly closed and healed, leaving not a scar on his god-like body. Karna faced the sun and finished his prayers. He neither repined nor regretted his act.

The chataka bird

• *Illustrated by Pulak Biswas* •

When summer comes to the hills and dries up all the grasses and lights fires in the forest, the sad, keening cry of a bird echoes in the hills and vales. The mountain folk will tell you it is the chataka, crying for water. And, if you ask, they will tell you the chataka's tale.

A long time ago, they say, in the valley below there lived a woman who had one daughter and one daughter-in-law. Both the girls had a pair of buffaloes each and everyday they drove them to the fields to plough the fields. One blazing summer day when the blue of the skies hurt the eyes, the bullocks, drained of all strength, slowly sank to the ground. The girls goaded the beasts with sticks but the bullocks were too tired to move. Then on the wind they heard drums and flutes and conches. There was a fair in the village! The girls forgot about their buffaloes and half-tilled fields. They jumped up bright-eyed with excitement.

'Let's go to the mela,' cried the daughter.

'We must ask mother first,' the daughter-in-law said.

And so the girls ran home. 'Mother there's a mela in the village!' cried the daughter. 'May we go?'

'Yes, but go back to the fields, water the bullocks and bring them home. And whoever returns first will get a large bowl of kheer,' the old lady said with a smile.

The girls raced back to the fields. They prodded and goaded the animals but the beasts wouldn't rise, not even to go down to the pond for a drink. After a few attempts the daughter gave up and went home. When her mother saw her she thought her daughter had watered the buffaloes and brought them home. 'Good girl,'

she said patting her head. 'Come and eat your kheer, and then you can go to the fair.'

The sly, lying creature ate the delicious kheer, changed into her festive clothes and went to the fair.

The daughter-in-law patiently kept prodding her bullocks till they rose. Then she led them down to the pond for a drink. When they were done she drove them home. It was almost dark when she got there.

'You've been out all day! Did it take so long to water your buffaloes?' the old woman said, annoyed. 'My daughter returned hours ago. Since you're late you shall not go to the fair.'

The daughter-in-law who was a nice girl didn't tattle—she didn't tell the old woman that her daughter hadn't watered her animals or brought them back.

That night the daughter's buffaloes died of thirst but before they died they laid a curse on her. 'In your next life you will be a bird, always thirsting for water. Only raindrops will quench your thirst.'

When the girl died she become a chataka and till the rains come to the hills it cries and it cries, waiting for the grey clouds to cloak the skies so that it can quench its thirst.

The brahmin and the goat

• Illustrated by Atanu Roy •

In a certain village there once lived a brahmin named Mitra Sharma whose chief duty was to keep the sacred fire burning at all times. One cold winter day, when a fine drizzle was falling and a sharp wind cut the air, the brahmin went to the next village to beg for an animal to sacrifice, as was the custom in those times. Walking through the lanes, he came upon a rich man's house and went in. 'I am performing a puja to the god of the moon. Give me an animal to offer the god.'

As the sacred books commanded, the rich man gave the brahmin a plump little beast. The brahmin checked it for blemishes and finding none, thanked the rich man and started back with the little animal.

The little goat, for a goat it was, pranced about darting here and there in the forest as little goats do. The brahmin, tired of chasing after it, decided to carry it. He picked up the goat, hoisted it onto his shoulders, and walked on.

He hadn't gone far when three cunning rogues chanced to see him; they also saw the plump little goat on his back. The thieves were very hungry and it was cold and wet. 'If we can somehow lay our hands on that goat, our bellies will be warm and full,' one muttered.

'It's a cold, miserable day. A hot mutton curry will keep the cold away,' said another.

The three thieves looked at each other in understanding, and smiles broke out on their faces. 'We'll trick the brahmin into parting with the animal!'

The brahmin walking down the forest path saw a man step out of the trees. The man's eyes were wide with shock. 'O, sir brahmin! What are you doing—carrying a dirty dog on your shoulders? You know brahmins shouldn't carry dogs.'

The brahmin was furious. 'Are you blind?' he snapped. 'Can't you see it's a goat?'

'Please don't get angry with me, sir,' said the first thief respectfully. 'I'm only telling you what I see,' he said and left.

A little further, the second rogue stepped out in front of the brahmin exclaiming, 'Your honour, how can you do such a thing? Your dead calf may have been your pride and joy but you shouldn't carry a dead beast on your shoulders. You'll become unclean!'

The brahmin's anger rose again. 'You idiot! Does this goat look like a dead calf?'

'Your holiness, I'm only telling you what I see. Please don't be angry,' the rogue said and went away.

A little later the third rogue stepped onto the path, a look of horror on his face. 'My good sir, what a terrible thing to do! How can you carry a donkey on your shoulders? You'd better throw it down before anyone sees you,' he said.

The poor brahmin was terrified now. 'This goat must be a demon! One man thought it was a dog, another thought it was a dead calf and now this man sees a donkey!' Shuddering, he flung the goat down and scampered back to his village.

The three rogues looked at his fleeing figure and laughed till their sides hurt. 'Ho! Ho! Ha! Ha! We fooled that stupid brahmin!'

Picking up the little goat they went into the forest and had a merry feast.

The death of Abhimanyu

• Illustrated by Usha Biswas •

The great war between the Kauravas and Pandavas lasted for eighteen long terrible days and millions died because of Duryodhana's greed and envy. But the saddest death was that of Abhimanyu, Arjuna's sixteen-year-old son.

After Bhishma was felled, the rules of war were thrown out on the rubbish heap and no codes guided conduct. Treachery became the order of the day and so the horrors multiplied tenfold. Drona now took command of the Kaurava armies and first tried to capture Yudhishthira, but could not. The next day Drona arranged his troops in the chakravyuha, the complex circular formation. Only a handful of people knew how to breach and break this formation. Among the Pandava generals, Arjuna was the only one, and he was far away, fighting on another front.

When Yudhishthira saw the Kauravas arranged in the chakravyuha, his heart sank. 'Today we will surely lose,' he said to the generals gathered in his tent. 'Bhima and the twins must try to make a breach.'

The three Pandavas led their forces and tried half a dozen times but failed and many lives were lost. Yudhishthira had only one option now, something he was very reluctant to do, but he was left with no choice. 'Fetch Abhimanyu,' the king said to a guard.

The faces in the tent grew grave but nobody protested. A few moments later Abhimanyu entered and bowed to his elders. 'You sent for me, father,' he said to Yudhishthira.

'Yes, my child, and what I am going to ask of you will take all your courage and skill,' the king said heavily. 'You are young and yet I am going to ask you to shoulder the responsibility of a seasoned warrior. Drona has his troops in the chakravyuha and only four men know its secrets. Of the four, Krishna, your father Arjuna and Krishna's son are not here. That leaves you. I need you to penetrate that foundation.'

'I can penetrate it all right but my father only had time to teach me how to enter, he didn't have time to teach me how to get out.' Abhimanyu wasn't afraid, he was simply pointing out facts. 'If the troops behind me are cut off, I'll be totally isolated,' he added matter-of-factly.

The elders knew if that happened Abhimanyu wouldn't live to see another day. Abhimanyu knew that too but that wasn't going to hold him back. In fact it would never have occurred to him to refuse.

'The rear-guard will be close behind,' Yudhishthira said. 'The men have been handpicked and are waiting.'

'Why am I here then?' Abhimanyu asked with a boyish laugh as he walked out of the tent, resolve in every line of his young body.

The young prince led his troops against forces commanded by some of the most experienced, battle-hardened warriors in the land. He led his troops in a curving sweep around the Kaurava forces to the weak link in the formation. His charioteer, driving hard and fast, broke the enemy ranks and shot through the elephant cordon with lightning speed, while Abhimanyu's arrows struck down everything in his path. As they raced towards the centre, the Kaurava troops sealed the breach cutting off his rear-guard which included Bhima, Krishna's cousin Satyaki and Draupadi's brother, the Prince of Panchala. Now he was all alone, surrounded by the enemy troops with no hope of breaking out. But the young prince had no time to waste on worrying about that. Duryodhana and his evil brother Dhushasana attacked him and he coolly parried their blows. Karna and the mighty Salya were so badly wounded by his arrows, they had to leave the field. When Drona saw the young warrior his eyes filled with love and admiration. Abhimanyu was a match for these experienced men. 'Arjuna's son is all alone and cut off and does he show a trace of fear?' he said to Kripa. 'Look at the dead that lie around him!'

Abhimanyu cut down the Kauravas like the scythe cuts grass for fodder. 'Close in and kill him!' Duryodhana shouted to his men. 'He's done enough damage.'

The surrounding Kauravas rained arrows on the lone youth but Abhimanyu ignored the feathered shafts sticking out of his body. As arrows flew thick and fast, Dhushasana fell on him like a raging beast. Abhimanyu smiled thinly when he saw him. 'Call yourself a warrior! You're only fit to attack women,' he taunted softly. 'You dragged my mother into court by her hair and then tried to strip her. Today I'll avenge Draupadi!'

So fierce was the attack that Dhushasana, seriously wounded, swooned and Abhimanyu leapt forward to strike the deathblow. But Dhushasana's charioteer swiftly turned the chariot and carried his master to safety. Abhimanyu swore under his breath.

The battle raged on and many a mighty warrior felt the bite of Abhimanyu's arrows. 'How do we kill him?' Karna cried to Drona, 'He's decimating us!'

Drona threw him a scornful look, his eyes glittering with anger. 'Can't you mighty warriors get past that boy's guard? His eye is unerring and his hands faster than lightning. Can you see them place the arrow and draw back the bowstring? No,' he answered for them, his lips curling disdainfully.

'How do we kill him?' Karna repeated angrily.

'Disarm him completely and cut off the armour,' Drona told him with cold dislike.

Six mighty warriors surrounded the young boy whose handsome face shone in spite of being covered by battle-dust. Some killed his charioteer and horses and broke his bow while others rained arrows on him. They broke his sword and then his mace but not before they had felt its bite. Left with no other weapon, Abhimanyu tore off a wheel from the chariot and rushed at his enemies, his long curling hair streaming in the wind. But the wheel was soon broken and the mighty warriors closed in. Abhimanyu staggered under the next volley of arrows, his battered wounded body could take no more punishment. Dazed with pain his legs buckled and he fell down on the dusty plain. Dhushasana's son struck him on the head with his mace and Abhimanyu lay still. The earth rose to pillow the young prince whose beautiful face shone like the moon even in death. He looked as if he was asleep. A breeze stirred the dusty curling locks and they moved as if there was still life. 'Six against one!' voices from the sky cried out. 'A deed most foul!'

The six great warriors stood looking down at the dead youth with shame in their eyes. They had only one desire now—that the war should not spare them. They could not bear the shame of being known as the killers of brave, young Abhimanyu.

The making of a king's jester

• *Illustrated by Krupa Thimmaiah* •

Long ago, in a small village in the mighty kingdom of Vijaynagar there lived a clever brahmin boy called Rama. One day, wandering aimlessly around the village the boy met a monk who was greatly impressed by the lad's intelligent face.

'Boy, come here!' he called. Rama strolled across and bowed briefly.

The monk looked intently into his bright, unafraid eyed and gave a satisfied nod. 'Right. I'm going to teach you a very powerful mantra which perhaps you will use well. If you recite this mantra thirty lakh times, you'll invoke the goddess Kali with her thousand fearful faces. When she appears you can ask her for a boon and she will have to grant it. Just don't let her scare you away.'

The monk recited the mantra, made Rama repeat it a dozen times and went on his way.

One day when the stars were in the right positions, Rama went to Kali's temple and began to chant. He stayed in the temple for days, chanting till he almost lost count. His mouth grew dry and his throat hurt and just when he thought he could chant no more he uttered the final mantra. Thunder rumbled and lightning tore through the clear, starry sky and a cold wind lashed the trees. Then suddenly all was calm and a glowing Kali stood before the boy.

Rama stared at the goddess' thousand faces, her red-rimmed eyes and two arms. The look was one of frank curiosity, not fear, and then, to the goddess' astonishment, a gale of laughter exploded and the boy rolled on the ground hugging his stomach. The affronted goddess blazed with anger; no one had laughed at her, not in a million

years. Usually, when she appeared people collapsed with fear. 'You cheeky, precocious little brat! How dare you laugh at me!' Kali said with a grim look.

'O Mother, I didn't mean to,' Rama said wiping his eyes, 'but when I saw you a really funny thought popped into my head.' And that set him laughing again.

'And what was that funny thought?' Kali snapped.

'W-e-l-l, we humans have just one nose and two hands and have enough trouble wiping it when we catch a cold,' said Rama grinning. 'I simply wondered how you managed a thousand running noses with just two hands.'

The goddess was livid. Her two thousand red-rimmed eyes blazed with anger. 'You will become a vikatakavi, a buffoon, and make your living through laughter.'

Instead of trembling with fear, Rama cocked his head as he pondered on the word. 'Vi-ka-ta-ka-vi,' he said slowly and then his expression brightened. 'Why that's a palindrome. It reads the same, back to front and front to back—you are clever,' he added admiringly.

Even a goddess can be charmed by genuine admiration. Kali's fury vanished and she almost grinned. 'Your wit and courage please me, you can see the funny side even in a curse. Much as I would like to, I cannot revoke it, but I can and will amend it. You will indeed be a jester, but a jester to a king,' she pronounced and vanished.

And so it came to pass. Tenali Rama as he was called, became the court jester of Krishnadevaraya, the great king of Vijaynagar.